Also by Elena Louise Richmond

---

99 Girdles on the Wall

a memoir about holding in, letting go, and coming to grips.

Advancing the Retreat

a Comedy

by

Elena Louise Richmond

Book and cover design:
Vladimir Verano
VertVolta Design + Press, vertvoltapress.com

Cover artwork © Elena Louise Richmond

Print: 978-1-7325738-0-2

ebook: 978-1-7325738-1-9

Published by

Elena Louise Richmond

Author contact:

www.elenalouiserichmond.com

ElenaRich@gmail.com

for Debi

With thanks for your encouragement and for your assessment of fiction versus memoir: it's harder to make things up from scratch than to lie about what happened in the first place.

This is a work of fiction. The Seattle locations are real but used fictitiously. There is a Crown Hill Community Church, but it is not on Dibble Avenue and the author has no experience of it. All characters and situations come from the author's imagination. Any resemblance to actual people or events is coincidental.

Dramatis Personae

The Narrators

April March—*married to Bob, mother of Nicholas, wants nothing more than to be left alone in her garden*

Mrs. Kimberly May Kendrick Cummings—T*he Pastor's Wife, who would have made the better pastor*

Chalice Martin—*cellist, church choir director, mystic wannabe, married to Kirk, mother of Chase*

Libby Cornish—*artist, new friend of April, newly divorced, new to the neighborhood*

The Ouroboros—*aka Omniscient Narrator*

The Church Folk

The Rev. Victor Ronald Cummings—*pastor of Crown Hill Community Church*

Bob March—*married to April, father of Nicholas, history teacher, born mentor*

Kay Groves—*church elder with excess energy, ideas, and common sense*

Jeff Schoenfield—*jazz pianist, church organist*

Esme—*almost useless church administrator*

Corinne—*gum-popping, quirky-dressing, blurt-outing, laugh-cackling owner of Marvin*

Brianna Carpenter—*seventeen years old, with as many piercings, adolescing nicely*

Wanda Carpenter—*Brianna's mother, with Coach bag grafted to her arm*

Mrs. Fred Johansen II—*known as Muffy, married to Fred*

Gwen Pennant—*photographer, dresses in black and white with one accent color*

Kirk Martin—*Mr. Mom, married to Chalice, father of Chase*

Chase Martin—*five years old, boing, boing, boing, boing, boing*

Nicholas March—*sophomore at Whitman College in Walla Walla, WA, son of April and Bob*

The Choir

Sopranos: *Brianna Carpenter, Madelaine McGuffin, Amanda*

Altos: *Gwen Pennant, Wanda Carpenter*

Tenors: *Bob March, Fred Johansen II (deaf in one ear)*

Bass: *Monty McDougal, Susan Moore, Nicholas when he's home from college, Jeff from the organ*

A Few Stray Supernumeraries

Sheila—*unhappy transplant from the Carolinas*

Danny—*grandson of the Johansens and owner of High Noon Pest Control*

Jerry—*Kay's son, who helps her with the flamboyant liturgical displays*

The Animals

Rambles—*April's orange tabby cat*

Marvin—*Corinne's miniature pinscher*

Callie—*Libby's Border collie*

And Coming From Out of Nowhere

Maxine—*the mysterious wise woman*

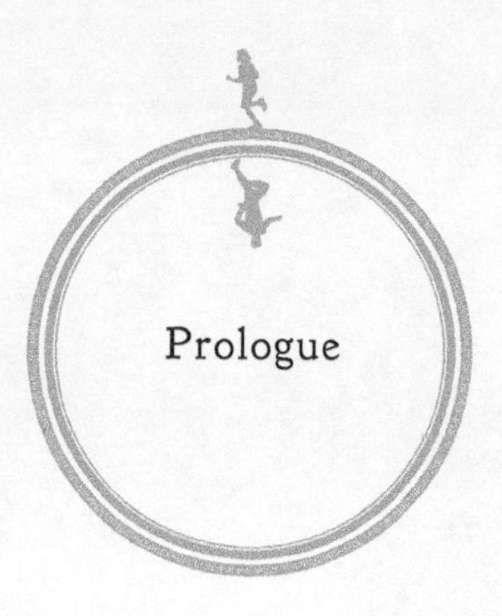

Prologue

People ought to stop aspiring to be other than human. It's not as though they've got the great mystery sorted out and can move on to more advanced subjects. Rather than interfere with earth or worse, take their business elsewhere in the universe, human beings could see themselves as creatures in a cycle of life and death and call it a day. They have the seasons to instruct them. Major religions have developed from the trope that life arises from death. Ashes to ashes. The circle is the oldest symbol that exists. Like the snake that eats its own tail. Like the Ouroboros. They won't call it a day. Ever was. Ever will be.

Part I: SEPTEMBER

Chapter One

April, Chalice, Kimberly, Libby

April March lay on the ground amongst her dahlias, her chin on a pile of chicken manure. She peered through the stems of her cutting garden, wondering how much longer she would be here. Labor Day weekend and Dibble Avenue's maple trees were already turning. Dog walkers that regularly passed the March home were already kicking and crunching their way through dead leaves in the countrified north end of Seattle, where there are no sidewalks. April held her breath when the labradoodles from down the street stopped on the parking strip to sniff. A couple of romping dogs calling attention to a middle-aged woman hiding in foliage was the last thing she wanted. Besides, their owner talked too much.

April had laid out a day of assiduous gardening. Her garden took up half a city lot to the side of the house. It was bounded by a weather-beaten and unpainted picket fence and featured paths that meandered through terraced levels of cruciferous vegetables and tomatoes (five different cultivars). Kohlrabi zoomed like little spaceships amongst the carrots and squashes. Flowering in the cutting garden were dahlias, stocks, sunflowers, and amaryllis (better known as naked ladies), mixing with asters and mums in a rumpled quilt of autumn color. Three-part harmony arose from the bee balm. Fruit trees stood in the corners of the garden like four old-fashioned bed posts: Italian prune, Spartan apple, Santa Rosa plum, and a tree with four grafted cultivars called a Cherry Bomb.

April's green plaid shirt hung off a shovel propped against the clerodendron (glory-bower) and her sun hat flopped on the ground next to a water bottle. Dripping soaker hoses jutted out of the ground. Homemade mulch baked on sheets of black plastic. A wet hose snaked around trays of winter pansies, kale, and mustard. Near a sliding glass door, pots of newly watered geraniums were lined up like soldiers ready to be marched into their winter quarters in the sunroom. By the front gate, stalks of crabgrass hung out of an open yard-waste container. Ropes of morning glory reached toward the crabgrass from a separate can, the private prison in which they were quarantined. April didn't want them in her compost.

April held her breath again when The Reverend Victor Ronald Cummings, the pastor of Crown Hill Community Church, which for better or worse was across the street from the March house, fiddled with the latch on the front gate and entered April's yard. Apart from not wanting to be distracted from her garden, she particularly did not want to cope with Victor. She watched him sidestep a morning glory vine prepared to strangle the life out of anything it could get its tendrils around. He scanned the yard, where two rosy finches took turns splashing the water of the bird bath. An orange cat sat two feet away, not looking at the birds, but staring through the dahlias into the eyes of the relevant party.

A shout from the church across the street turned Victor around. He hurried out the front gate, leaving it swinging open. A piece of morning glory vine managed to get ahold of him and ride across the street to the church, where a figure blocked his entrance to the side door.

She turned her head at a rustle in the dahlias. The orange cat stepped delicately through the forest of stems to where she lay, manure beginning to seep down her neck.

"I'm better than this, Rambles," April said.

She and the cat looked at each other. Then the cat backed out of the flower bed, did a turn around the now empty bird-bath, and wandered toward the sunroom, taking a desultory swipe at a butterfly on the way.

April explored her position and tentatively raised herself up on one elbow. She rotated a hip. Pushing carefully so as not to wound any of the garden residents, she turned herself onto her knees. She stood up in increments, peering across the street over the tops of the dahlias as she did so. She could see the pastor in the church's side door and the arm of someone shaking a fistful of papers. April could hear tones, but not content, although she caught the word "can't" several times.

April crouched down so as to be out of sight while she had a think. Damn. Her whole morning was now taken hostage by the pastor. Until he (in his secondhand Cadillac, license plate DOCDIV left the neighborhood, it wasn't safe to be in her own yard. She bent low, shook manure and garden debris out of her curly hair, and scrambled into the sunroom, which took her into the kitchen at the back of the house.

Rambles was waiting in the kitchen sink.

"You want sumpin' to drink?" April cooed.

Rambles narrowed his eyes.

April stationed herself at a window of the breakfast nook, which offered a view of the church's side door. Rambles' eyes burned two holes into her face, where an indeterminate slimy thing from the garden had left a streak.

Her husband, Bob, a Whitman College cap on his head, sat at the kitchen table putting on bicycle shoes. He got up, clonked experimentally on each foot, hitched at his chamois crotch, and ran a stream of water for Rambles. "What's going on?"

"Victor," said April. "He's energy draining and soul destroying."

"I'm off. Last sixty miles before school starts." Bob squeezed April's shoulders and wiped chicken manure off his hands onto the back of her T-shirt. "He's not that bad," he stage-whispered.

Rambles' pink tongue lizarded in and out of the running water. He paused, let the water meter tick away, and then resumed sipping. Finally he jumped out of the sink and sat beside his bowl on the floor.

April washed her hands, turned off the stream of water, dropped two green fish crackers in his dish, and went back to her post at the window. Her husband was born a mentor. Or an uncle. He was beloved by his students. April suspected that he was drawn to Victor because Victor was a lost soul who needed mentoring. Her hands freed the back hooks of her brassiere and, with a few contortions of her shoulders, she pulled the bra out one of her sleeves.

April had been slim and wiry as a young adult, but after the birth of her son she grew a belly, a butt, and more breasts than she knew what to do with. The necessity of a bra personally affronted her. When she came in the house after a morning of turning the earth and heaving around compost, she ripped off her bra and hung it over the caps and jackets inside the pantry door.

The church's side door closed. April's eyes roamed over the piles of mulch and trays of starts in her yard. She could feel the chickweed maturing amongst the tomatillos. Her hands felt sticky with the anticipation of yanking out the nasty stuff.

Bob set off down Dibble Avenue toward 87th but stopped in the traffic circle to chat with someone. The phone rang. April looked at it. Kay. It was Kay's voice April had heard earlier shrieking "can't." Kay must be subbing in the church office that morning.

April picked up. "What's going on over there?"

"Victor. He shouldn't be allowed to control the petty cash. There's nothing to give Danny when he comes to check the traps."

"For the rats?"

"Whatever. Listen, can you come over for a minute? I'm stuck here until little Miss Esme gets back from her dentist appointment."

"Can't. I'm hiding from Victor."

"I figured. He's leaving in a few minutes. Kimberly just ordered him home. I'll call you when he goes."

"Don't bother. I'll know."

"OK, honey."

April smiled. "I have a friend who calls me honey," she thought.

The friendship with Kay aside, buying a house across the street from Crown Hill Comm had seemed merely a nuisance fifteen years ago. It became a bad joke when Bob wanted to become a member a decade later.

"I can see where you might go once in a while, but why do you have to join?" April had asked.

"I want to see what it's like."

"Can't you see what it's like without committing yourself?"

"It's not an asylum."

"You don't know that."

When Bob joined and had his little moment of installation — April called it his insanity hearing — in front of the congregation, she sat in the back pew and watched. With Bob as a member, Victor had presumed a license to pursue April with his hands full of flyers about new members' classes. She was as polite in her refusals as she knew how to be, politeness not being one of her strong points. April taught at a community college. She was used to having students in her face. She knew how to make a mark and tell them not to cross it. But Victor didn't seem to think normal human boundaries applied to him. He also talked too much. All April wanted was to be left alone in her garden.

Nicholas's ring sounded on her phone.

"Are you coming home for Thanksgiving?"

"Hi, Mom."

"Hi. Well?"

"I think so."

"What can I do to entice you?"

"Don't make me go anywhere or invite anyone else to our house. Or at least give me veto power."

"You should say that to your father. He's the generous one. How are your classes?"

"OK. I think I'm going to like the American Novel."

April saw license plate DOCDIV coming up the church's side alley.

"Gotta go, sweetheart, unless there was something else?"

"Nope, just calling to say hello as you ordered."

April watched Victor's Cadillac turn south. Then she clomped in her garden boots through the sunroom door and down the side of the yard. By her front gate, she pushed the morning glory vines farther into their quarantine, squished some aphids on a new rose growth, latched the gate behind her, and crossed the street to the church. In the traffic circle at 87th and Dibble Avenue, Bob was still talking to someone. A girl. Probably one of his history students. Bob, the mentor. April had a more perfunctory approach to her community college students. God knew they could all use some mentoring but April's patience was reserved for plants. She went through the church's side door.

In the church office, Kay had created padding and support from some green velvet swag to prop herself up in the desk chair, her elbow on a wad of twenty-dollar bills and her gray head bent over a crossword puzzle book. She looked up and stared through April.

"What?" April asked.

"Twenty-two down, a five-letter word that means pretentious."

"I came over for this?"

Kay blinked. She let her reading glasses drop on their button-and-rhinestone chain to her bosom. "No," she said. "This."

Using the cash as a bookmark, she closed her crosswords and handed April a lavender folder. Inside was a glossy photograph of a woman in her late twenties, clearly naked but holding sheet music in such a way as to obscure all but a hint of décolletage and a titillating roundness protruding from the bottom of the music. Behind her were deep orange and black flames. The caption read, "What it takes to get the choir to watch me."

"Wow," said April admiringly. "I'm surprised Chalice agreed to this."

"She doesn't know about the flames. Gwen put them in. What's 'Photoshop' mean? No, don't tell me. I don't care. This should be for January. I have an idea for one of the summer months, which we can do now if we get to it before your hydrangea fades. You keep this one where it's safe."

April smiled. Kay didn't know about jpgs, hard drives, or even email. At seventy-eight, she was a battery charger looking for a battery. April thought she would have made a kick-ass grandmother but neither of her sons had seen fit to give her grandchildren. She had been a PTA president and a den mother. She had sewn the costumes for fifteen school plays, setting a record. She had run bake sales, book sales, and holiday gift-wrapping services. She had sat on the Interfaith Advisory Council and the AIDS Outreach Center board. She changed all the displays for the church liturgical seasons, which explained why she had access to green velvet. She catered memorials and receptions. There was no end to what she could do for her family, her church, her neighborhood, and the world. But the world had gone digital and she didn't know what that meant.

April and Kay had met over April's garden fence years earlier, that being much the only way a person could meet April. Kay had steamed out of the church and crossed the street to breathe heavily through her nose and stare at April's gooseberries.

"Pastor Toady," she had muttered. "Calling me a pillar of the church. Pillars aren't alive. They just stand there and people ignore them. I refuse to be a pillar."

"Then I won't ask you to hold this beanpole," replied April from under the fence.

They had hatched the calendar idea early in the summer. April had agreed to supply the church with flowers from her garden for the upcoming year and had grudgingly attended the council meeting when the arrangement came under discussion. She and Kay stared across the council table at each other while Mrs. Kimberly May Kendrick Cummings, the pastor's wife, droned on about the fund-raising conference she had just attended. April muttered that it sounded unbearably dreary.

"It's hard work," Kimberly said. "You don't do it to have fun."

"Clearly," said April.

Kay snorted.

Kimberly glared.

After the meeting, Kay and April huddled. Out of that huddle had come the idea of creating an irreligious calendar, something to prod the sacred cows that snored through religious culture. All those churchy things that people pretended to care about because they knew they were expected to but had long since forgotten why.

"Victor is in a lather about the calendar." Kay opened her crossword book and moved aside her cash bookmark. "He's trying to discourage it because he says money for a small church comes from members' pledges. As though he'd refuse the money if the calendar made any. More to the point, as though we have enough members to keep this place afloat."

"What's that cash you've got there?"

"It's to pay the pest guy. Victor had to take it out of his wallet because the petty cash is gone. He thinks someone is pilfering. Help me: a five-letter word that means pretentious and ends in a *y*."

The side door opened to a tall, skinny woman in a floor-length black skirt and a red and yellow peasant blouse. As she swanned into the office, she twisted her stringy, mucous-colored hair into a bun at the back of her head, her capacious yellow bag banging against a hip-bone, her mouth full of pins and clasps.

"I'm back," Esme announced.

April watched over Kay's shoulder as she filled in the five-letter word: *phony*.

When April left the church and crossed to her fence, Bob and the girl were still in the traffic circle. April hallooed and they both turned.

"Oh, nuts," thought April. "I forgot about Brianna."

Rambles came through a widening in the fence and wound around April's legs. She picked him up. Brianna detached herself and headed toward her. Bob waved, threw a leg over his bike, and pedaled off in the other direction.

Brianna stopped at the fence and saluted. "Here to heel in the Lysistrata, *Sir.*"

April laughed. "There's been a change of plans."

The decision was made as the words came out. Rambles jumped down from April's arms and stalked off.

"Thank God! We're going for mani-pedis instead of shoveling that shit out there?"

"I found someone whose needs you might find more congenial than mine. Let me give her a call and see if we can go over. And that's mulch, not manure. Come on in."

Brianna was seventeen years old, with almost as many piercings. Five years ago, when Bob became a church member, Brianna confided to April that she had refused to go through confirmation classes. Sensing a fellow traveler, April had made it her business to befriend the girl and, to that end, had offered her a job working in the garden. She didn't withhold her irreligious observations when the two of them were seeding the lettuce or planting the onion sets or moving around the shoots of Kerria japonica.

"That church is a clutch of eggs," April had said. "An enclosed bunch of embryos, some of them cracked, some of them hatched and chirping, a few of them fully cooked."

Now Brianna sat in the sunroom, scrolling down her cell phone. April called from the kitchen. "Libby says we can come over now. I need to pee, then we'll be off." She left the bathroom door ajar.

"Who's Libby?" Brianna went into the kitchen.

On the refrigerator was a photo of Nicholas at Whitman College. He was standing in the wind and sunshine of Ankeny Field, his cheeks glowing and his curly hair dancing across his forehead.

"Someone in the neighborhood I met this summer. She was on crutches and had come as far as my house on one of her first forays out."

April came out of the bathroom in time to see Brianna click her phone at the refrigerator door.

"Is Nicholas coming home for Thanksgiving?"

April looked at the photo of her son. "I think so." She looked thoughtfully at Brianna.

"Why is she on crutches?"

"What? Umm, car accident. She broke her leg. You'll like her. Your mother will hate her."

"Good. Let's go."

Rambles followed April and Brianna down Dibble Avenue and across 87th until they entered the driveway of a small renovated Cape Cod. Rambles sniffed around cautiously, then retreated across the street to the traffic circle, where his orange fur became one with the autumn colors. He curled up and fell asleep.

The woman who opened the door to April and Brianna was in her late forties, her brown hair in a pageboy cut, her brown eyes behind rimless glasses in a design just interesting enough that they couldn't be termed granny glasses. Her leg boot bulged out of the ripped side of a long, dark blue, paisley skirt. Over a white tank top she had wrapped herself in a voluminous blue sweater, one sleeve quite obviously shorter than the other. A black and white Border Collie pressed up against her good leg, his tail wagging energetically as he barked at the new arrivals.

"This is Callie. Come on in." She looked at Brianna. "Hi, I'm Libby."

"This is Brianna Carpenter," April said.

"Did you make your sweater?" Brianna asked.

"Yes. How can you tell?" Libby held both arms straight down, showing off the uneven sleeves. "It works for me because the shorter sleeve is on my dominant arm so that cuff never gets in my way."

Libby led her guests through a trail of packing crates and crumpled newsprint. Callie's tail thumped against boxes as she followed Libby, sending little explosions of packing peanuts into the air. When she turned a full circle to check on the visitors, her tail picked up the sticky tape on some bubble wrap, which she subsequently wagged into the front room. Brianna and April picked their way to a windowed corner, where a little nest of domesticity had been built around a couch and a desk.

A dining table was covered with small, partially unpacked boxes and a bowl of apples. A collection of vases stood solemnly like standing stones next to a stack of books. A pitcher of amber liquid and a glass sat on a single placemat. Next to the table was a small drinks cart, on which a stack of newspapers were soaking up a pile of sopping tea bags.

Libby rescued the bubble wrap from the dog's fur. She used a crutch to push boxes off the couch and invited her guests to sit. Callie did a lap around the couch and, with a grunt, settled on the floor next to Libby, who sat in her desk chair and laid her crutches down.

Brianna flounced onto the couch but April leaned over Libby's desk, which faced Dibble Avenue and the traffic circle, where Rambles was asleep in a pile of lobelia. She could see her cat, a small bright lion resting on a dark blue carpet. She spotted her sunflowers a block north and wondered if some late blooming, dark blue delphiniums might set off their yellow. Or maybe asters. It was hard to find anything that grew as high as sunflowers.

"Would you like something to drink?" Libby asked.

"Sure." April turned from the window. "We can get it."

"That's probably the fastest. That stuff on the table is sun tea that I made this morning. It's still warm but there's ice in the fridge. You'll have to rummage for glasses. There's this one and one by the sink. The box they came from is somewhere. My sister was here for a while but she was on a diet and afraid to spend any time in the kitchen so a lot didn't get unpacked."

"I'll rummage. You and Brianna talk."

Libby and Brianna looked at each other while April pawed through packing material.

"I count fourteen earrings and one nose ring," Libby said. "Is it rude to count?"

"I actually have a belly button piercing, too. Do you want to see it?"

"Love to."

Brianna pulled up her T-shirt.

"And a tattoo," Libby murmured. "Was that legal?"

"No. But I know a guy."

"Let's see." April came over. "Wow, does Wanda know?"

"After the fact. I was grounded pretty much for life. And she tried to make me go through confirmation classes again."

"And you got out of it again."

"I said I'd sing in the choir."

"You're from the church down the block?" Libby asked. "I noticed a lot of construction activity when I first moved in."

"They've built a new wing and there's going to be a labyrinth."

"Tell Libby what they named the project." April dug into another box.

"The pastor is big on not very clever names for the things he starts but never finishes. It's called the 'Advancing the Retreat Project.'"

"What does that mean?"

"The idea was to build a wing and a labyrinth that could be used by outside groups for retreats. When it was in its planning stages, he was *advancing* the idea for *a retreat* center. Get it? It's what I call *aclever*."

"The labyrinth is a nice touch, though," Libby said. "Churches are always trying to get bigger instead of going deeper. A labyrinth seems like a step into depth."

"How so?"

"It's a contemplative activity. You walk along a kind of maze. People can do whatever they want with the experience, but I like to walk and let rise whatever thoughts come to me. When I get into the center, I notice what I'm thinking and again when I get to the end. Sometimes nothing remarkable comes of it. Sometimes questions I didn't know I had get answered. You don't really know what a labyrinth walk is for until you do it. Contemplation is not something much valued in our culture. Come to think of it, a labyrinth kind of advances a retreat. You end up where you started, only in a different place, if that makes any sense."

"Found the glasses!" April called through a great rustle of bubble wrap. "Shall I unpack them all for you?"

"No, just put a few in the kitchen and get some ice."

April threaded her way to the kitchen and came back with an ice tray and two glasses. She rattled and poured. "I've been thinking of putting a labyrinth in my garden."

Brianna grinned. "Get out. That would be a great big 'fuck you' to the church project."

April picked up the water glass on Libby's desk and emptied its contents into a sad-looking plant.

"This hoya is dehydrated," she informed no one who cared. She filled the glass with iced tea. "You sound like you know something about churches, Libby."

"I knew half a pastor once."

"What's half a pastor?" April passed a glass of iced tea to Brianna and sat down next to her.

"A divinity student. At Berkeley. We went out for a while. Then he disappeared."

"That's not much of a story," Brianna said. "What, did you sleep with him?"

"Yikes, Brianna. Reign in the curiosity til at least the second visit."

"It's okay, April. It was such a long time ago." Libby looked at Brianna. "Actually, yes. Back then there was an idea that a man lost all respect for a woman if he slept with her outside of marriage."

"Some of the Christians at school still say that. Well, their mothers say it."

"Do they still? I'm out of the game now. I've given up expecting religion to do anything good for women."

"April was right. My mother would hate you."

"Did you talk to April?"

Mrs. Kimberly May Kendrick Cummings, in her scrupulously appointed kitchen, had assembled cutting board, sharpening steel, knife, red onion, a heap of basil, and a pile of Roma tomatoes. Kimberly excelled at everything she did. Her Insalata Caprese was a celebrated staple of church potlucks.

"I couldn't find her." Victor hung his jacket over the back of a sturdy Ethan Allen chair.

"Kay and April are up to their ears in this calendar thing." Kimberly drew the knife across the steel.

"Why do you say that?"

"You've been so preoccupied with the construction that you've lost the pulse of everything else. Have you seen that?" Kimberly pointed with her sharpened knife at a postcard on the table. "It came in the mail just now."

Victor picked it up. On it was a drawing of a large circle, which upon closer inspection turned out to be a snake eating its own tail. Inside the snake-circle nine candles burned in an open hearth.

"That looks like Chalice's fireplace," he remarked.

"It *is* Chalice's fireplace. The card is from Chalice."

"Is she inviting us to some kind of party?"

Kimberly put down the knife, crossed the room, and snatched the card out of her husband's hand.

"'Ouroboros. The Endless Return. Explore your spiritual self and find your way home,'" she read. "What is this about?"

"Nothing. It doesn't have anything to do with the church."

"Then why did we get this?"

"Well, you know, that's just Chalice. She probably sent one to everyone she knows."

"She's also put an announcement in the church bulletin for this Sunday."

"How do you know that?"

"Esme told me. I was helping her with some of the admin stuff that she doesn't seem to grasp."

"When's lunch?"

Victor went through the living room to his study.

"We need to talk about the labyrinth," Kimberly called after him. "I don't see how we can afford it. We're past due two payments on the loan. Did you *know* that?"

Victor shut the study door.

Kimberly picked up the knife. She put it down again. She sat at the table. Her eyes narrowed and she sat for a long time with her chin in her hands. She chewed her lower lip and peeled away some skin.

She picked up an envelope that hadn't been part of the mail. Victor must have brought it in with him. It was labeled *Sermons*. Inside were two sheets of paper.

One looked like minutes from some kind of meeting. Wanda Carpenter had commented that the sermons this summer did not run over twenty minutes and that was a good thing. Mrs. Fred Johansen II had commented that in the sermon dated June 8, Victor had touched on no less than seventeen different topics in the course of a thirty-five minute sermon, none of which had anything to do with its title, "A Pillar of Salt." Mrs. Johansen still had no idea what the sermon was about or why it had been called "A Pillar of Salt." Monty McDougal suggested that Victor work with someone to help him improve his preaching because he didn't think the sermon committee was enough.

The second sheet was a handout that described — with diagrams — how to construct an outline. It was something Bob March gave his high school history class. There was a handwritten note: "I can help you with this."

Kimberly closed her eyes. She had been head of her debate team in college. She had majored in rhetoric studies and religion. She could construct an outline in her sleep. She had given talks to her conservative women's group, The Conservanteurs that sparkled in their succinctness.

Victor's sermons were lasting only twenty minutes because in Victor's preoccupation with the Advancing the Retreat Project, Kimberly had been editing them. She had been at the fundraising conference the week of the lengthy, seventeen-topic sermon of June 8 and hadn't gotten home in time to rescue it. She could only imagine the irrelevancies that Mrs. Fred Johansen II was referring to. Victor's mind was a scribble picture; he had to trace every line before settling on the larger shapes. It was a contrast to her disciplined intelligence. She tried to not think about the irony. She just saw what was in front of her and got on with it.

Kimberly would have made the better pastor. That, in fact, was the life she was working toward when she met Victor. Her unofficial presence in his life as the administrator in the Phoenix church where he was interning had morphed into her official presence as his wife. As such, her intelligence and her many leadership qualities were wrinkles that had to be ironed in the direction of supporting her husband. That was what women did.

Kimberly looked at Bob March's outline diagram. She had seen this diagram before. It brought back memories of a daughter who had been in Mr. March's history class at Nathan Hale High School, a daughter who no longer spoke to her, a daughter she hadn't heard from in four years. Not a day went by that she didn't look through the mail, hoping one of those envelopes or one of those emails would be from her daughter, Victoria. Today had been no different. Kimberly had rifled through the mail and instead found the postcard from Chalice.

She contemplated interrupting Victor in his study. Closing the door was his signal he didn't want to be disturbed. The supportive wife stood up, tapped the *Sermons* documents, and walked through the front room. She knocked on Victor's study door. There was no answer. Kimberly turned the knob and peeped in. Victor was asleep on the couch Kimberly had vacuumed that morning.

She dropped the two sheets of paper on Victor's desk and went back to the kitchen. She grabbed her purse and a Mariners baseball cap, abandoned the sliced tomatoes that were running all over the basil and onions, and left the house. She backed her Subaru out of the drive and pointed it north.

Victor wasn't asleep. Kimberly knew that Victor wasn't asleep. Victor knew that Kimberly knew that he wasn't asleep. Victor relied on the fragments of his well-being to remain stitched in place, like beans in a beanbag, with the reassurances of his wife, the approbation of the church Council, and the hugs and handshakes of his congregation. When a seam frayed, he could do a quick patch job as Kimberly had suggested he do that morning with April. Actually she had ordered him to. Currently there was too much pressure on the mechanism. Kimberly did an inventory of what was most likely on her husband's mind besides her own annoyance with him.

There was this calendar business. Kay and April, a dangerous pair in the smoothest of times, were plotting something lurid.

Kimberly had seen no actual photos, and, as far as she could gather, neither had Victor. His description of the calendar said a great deal about his own imagination and it had raised the council's collective eyebrows.

The labyrinth, in Kimberly's estimation, was a nuisance and an expense they didn't need. But since Victor wouldn't let go of it, it had to happen before the cold weather dampened everyone's enthusiasm, not that Kimberly had detected much of that. The church rat had more enthusiasm.

Then there was Chalice. Chalice was becoming A Concern. Victor wanted a music festival for the labyrinth dedication — a labyrinth that had yet to be laid. Kimberly recalled Chalice's response to the notion of a festival: incredulity that bordered on impudence. Privately, Kimberly was impressed with the young woman's pushback. This was her second year as choir director of Crown Hill Community Church. Victor had crowed that he ushered Chalice through her first year, directing her performance, so to speak. Kimberly's assessment had been that Chalice had seemed malleable that first year when, in fact, she was just new. Now she was not just questioning Victor's ideas about music. With this group she was proposing, she was crowding him on his own turf.

Kimberly suppressed a smile. She drove faster.

One end of the church vestry connected to the church office, the other to the choir loft of the sanctuary. It was a narrow room with a small toilet room and a large farmhouse sink. Traditionally a vestry housed the vicar's liturgical attire and communion paraphernalia. The vestry at Crown Hill Community Church was crammed with other things, principally choir robes that were never used, dusty folders of music, stained vases, and a collection of pagan-looking statues — naked babies and women — that came out in tableaux at Christmas and other holidays, trying to look more religious and less gay than they were. Kay's son Jerry had a flair for the flamboyant and the two of them enjoyed creating the liturgical season displays. So far no pastor had been able to stop them.

A long table stretched almost the length of the vestry. Chalice (self-named) Martin sat at one end. Her breasts in a low-cut purple top plopped on the table, a chain of rosary beads and an enormous pewter Venus between them. Her elbows propped up her hands, which were holding up her head. Bracelets stacked up her arms, rode her forearms, and clinked with every movement. Long earrings bumped against her hands as she rocked her head back and forth, staring at the piles of music in front of her. Cartons of yellowed choir folios lay in furrows of dust on the floor at her feet. She thought of the piece of cake she had eaten (yellow with penuche frosting) as a preemptive reward for what she had come here to do: go through the archives of old choir music to see if there was anything she could use not just for the coming year, but ever. There were two file cabinets full of the passé harmonies of the 1940s and 50s and the unrelentingly cheerful praise songs of the 1960s.

Also in front of her was a bottle of a viscous, slime-green drink and a vial of aspen flower essence drops. Chalice took a sip of her protein smoothie. After she finished this chore, maybe she'd take a nap. Tomorrow she would purge her house of sugar. She sniffed. The choir music smelled of damp. Everything in the Pacific Northwest smelled of damp. She should have the basement checked for dry rot. She wished she had brought a piece of cake with her.

From the direction of the sanctuary the sound of Bach's *Toccata and Fugue in D minor* stabbed the vestry with full force. The D minor toccata signaled that Jeff was on the premises and ready to make Church Music. It was his mental transition from jazz pianist to church organist.

"Jeff! Get in here!"

Jeff padded into the vestry in his stocking feet. "There's a hole in the wall out here. Did you see it?"

Chalice plopped a stack of music onto the floor. "No."

Jeff waved at the dust. "What are those?"

"The ones I can't use."

"Really?" He picked up a sheet and shook off an indeterminate insect that had died clinging to the title page. "What's wrong with this one? 'All in the April evening… little lambs.' It sounds nice."

"Keep reading."

"'All in the April evening…the lambs ….weak human cry… going meekly to die.' Oh dear." Jeff scratched his nose and skimmed the rest of the text.

"It was a hit in its day."

"Is there anything you can use?"

"Oh, one or two, maybe. Most of this music is fifty years old. If I see a *thee* or *thou* or *doth,* I figure it hath sung its swan song."

Jeff sat down. With his thumb and forefinger he held the wretched lambs above the pile on the floor and let them fall.

Chalice pushed a piece of music toward him. "Victor wants this. He seems to think we can build an entire music festival around it."

"'There Shall a Star Come out of Jacob,'" Jeff read formally. "By Felix Mendelssohn."

"He sang it in that choir he keeps on about."

"Oh, yes, the Auditioned Choir." Jeff continued reading. "'With might destroying princes and powers.' Well, it's a change from the angels and shepherds. Can you write a different text?"

"Oh, that's a thought. Something as warm as the harmonies. There are some lovely parts, really."

"The adolescents in the choir will never let you get away with 'a scepter shall rise out of Israel,'" Jeff said. "You'd definitely need to do something about that."

"Do something about what?" An armload of sunflowers, dahlias, and ferns came through the office door with April's face just visible through them. Under her arm was a lavender folder. She laid the flowers in the sink.

"Victor wants a music festival to open the new wing and show off the labyrinth," Chalice said. "Here it is, the end of August, but he wants something in October while it's still nice out and people can walk the labyrinth, which hasn't yet been laid. And he wants this Christmas piece. I don't understand how his mind works."

"His mind runs on anxiety. And he's trying to make everything be about that stupid retreat project thingy of his so he can get it paid for. Bob says Kimberly's all over him about it."

"Here. Look at this song." Jeff handed 'There Shall a Star Come out of Jacob' to April. "Victor wants us to create a music festival around this piece and I said we'd have to change the words."

April read the text.

"'And a scepter shall rise out of Israel,'" April read. "Erection. Change the words to something about the erection of the new wing."

"Just give me that. We're not doing it." Chalice twitched the music away from April and dropped it flat on the floor along with its thirty copies.

"Chalice, look at this." April opened the lavender folder and presented Chalice with the photo of her nakedness hiding behind choir music.

Jeff looked over her shoulder. "Wow, you're beautiful!"

"Am I?" All her life, Chalice had wondered if she could be beautiful without being thin. Because she was never going to be thin, especially not now that she had had a child. A good photograph of her did not exist; she hated them all. But this one, which was supposed to be a joke, wasn't bad. She could feel every centimeter of her hairline grow warm. More than anything she did not want anyone to know she had these thoughts, even though they preoccupied her much of the time.

A scratching from the direction of the office dispelled the moment. Chalice heard Esme's drone-y voice and another sound, a cackling laugh. A thump opened the door and produced a small creature that looked like a leather shoebox propelled by tiny legs. A small pointy head stuck out one end and a tiny tail wagged out the other. The leather dog jacket was festooned with feathers, silver charms, decals, and long irregularly cut fringe. The small body wriggled free of the outfit and jumped onto Jeff's lap, wagging its tail so hard that it fanned the choir music.

"Hiya, Marvin," said Jeff.

An apparition appeared in the doorway. She was dressed no less colorfully than her dog. From bottom to top were army boots, white athletic socks, green tights, Dockers, camouflage jacket open to reveal breasts about to bust their black tank top, orange crocheted scarf, and a Mariners baseball cap with feathers and charms to match the ones on Marvin's leather jacket. She was laboriously working her mouth around a huge wad of gum. Corinne.

Esme firmly closed the office door.

"Have they caught the rat yet?" Corinne demanded.

"I've no idea," said Jeff. "Something has chewed a hole in the wall behind the choir loft. Looks too big for rats."

"Min Pins are ratters," Corinne said. "I bet Marvin could find whatever it is. C'mon Marvin." She picked up the piece of leather that Marvin had escaped from. "Gonna have to move these hooks so his coat will stay on. He keeps walking me all over the city; we're both losing weight." Popping her gum, she went into the sanctuary to look at the hole in the wall.

"They do walk all over the city," April said. "I saw them out by Sky Nursery once. They started on the Interurban Trail at Northgate Way and just kept going."

Chalice slipped the photo of her décolletage back in the lavender folder and pushed it aside. She unscrewed the dropper of her aspen flower essence and put a few drops on her tongue.

She watched April turn back to the flowers in the sink and rummage in a drawer for the church's blunt secateurs.

Chalice sighed. An hour ago, she was sitting alone and quiet, able to think. Now there were people and flowers and dogs and rats and that woman in the office who really bothered her.

She took up a pile of music. "C'mon, let's read through these."

In the sanctuary, Jeff slid onto the organ bench and Chalice hitched up to the piano. The choir loft stretched across the nave between the piano and the organ. On the wall behind the piano, swathes of green unfurled from ceiling to floor, where they pooled as though waiting for a nude model to step into them. On the other side of the nave, two green swags were united with an indeterminate religious-looking symbol, rather like a woman's brooch pinned in the middle of her evening wrap.

Above the choir loft, under the swag and about where the basses stood, was a jagged hole the size of a fist. April, coming from the vestry with a vase of flowers, said, "That's not a rat hole."

Chalice and Jeff joined her. The three stood like statues contemplating the irreverent work of some rodent.

There was a loud, scratching sound in the wall.

All three involuntarily moved back a foot.

Marvin's head poked through the hole in the wall. When he saw his audience, he barked happily and a cackling laugh joined in.

"Corinne," called April. "What are you doing?"

"Just seeing if there's anything I can do about the hole." Corinne's voice was muffled. "I could probably cut some drywall to fill the hole and duct tape it on this side. Then we could hang that drape-y thing over it in front."

"Hello?" A male voice came from the direction of the church office.

Jeff disappeared into the vestry, grinning, and came back with a stocky man: Danny of High Noon Pest Control. His T-shirt read, "Your life as you know it is over." His baseball cap had a Playboy logo and behind one ear was a cigarette.

"The Rat Man cometh," Jeff announced.

High Noon Pest Control was actually just Danny, a trunk full of rat and mice traps, some jars of peanut butter, and a complicated telephone intake system. Danny was the ex-druggie grandson of church members Fred and Margaret Johansen II, which was why Victor had hired him to trap the rat. Also he worked cheap and was mollified with petty cash.

"Where is Esme?" asked Chalice. "Isn't she in charge of this?"

The toilet in the vestry flushed and Esme rushed into the sanctuary, the smell of cigarette smoke wafting before her.

Chalice sat down on the piano bench. She thought again about the cake at home.

By late afternoon Libby pronounced Brianna deft with the arrangement of the household gods and goods. The kitchen was unpacked and a broad path connected it to Libby's nest in the corner of the living room. All unpacked boxes were relegated to one corner and there wasn't a packing peanut in sight. Libby watched Brianna reverently inspect her books one at a time. They were now arranged by subject matter: poetry, spirituality, women authors, nonfiction.

The two of them were again seated in Libby's corner.

"Thank you, Brianna, for everything you've done today."

"That's okay."

"Have you lived in Seattle all your life?"

"I was born in Mexico."

"Were you?"

"My parents were missionaries."

"But they aren't anymore?"

"I guess my dad is somewhere down there with la esposa. I don't see him except when he comes up here."

"La esposa?"

"Wife."

"So he married someone else. I know how that goes. By now I would be back east with my ex but it turned out he had plans for a different female to accompany him." She waved her hands. "Enough of that. I bet you learned Spanish."

"I don't speak it up here."

"That makes sense."

"It does?"

"Yeah, I think so. When you learn a language as a child, it's a pragmatic thing. When you come home, the reason for speaking it is gone. You don't see it as a skill to maintain."

"My mom wanted me to take Spanish for my foreign language requirement but I took American Sign Language instead. She was really mad about that. Maybe sometime I'll tell you the whole story."

"Will you come back, then? Until I get out of this boot, I could use the help."

"Yeah, this is better than working at April's."

Brianna's phone buzzed. She read the text. "That's my mom. She's sitting outside April's house wondering where I am."

"Coming," Brianna texted.

Libby watched her pass the traffic circle. She looked at the tidy kitchen. She looked at her books organized in her book cases. The place was beginning to look like someone lived there. Libby wished she knew who that someone was.

She had known who she was the minute before she found the airline tickets to Logan International, one for her then husband and one for his assistant, Ms. Chantal LeBec. (Cringe-worthy name. She made it up, Libby thought.) With the airline ticket was the rental agreement for a townhouse in Boston. That was when Libby stopped knowing who she was and had to start getting acquainted with this stupid Libby who lived inside her. It was the stupid Libby who after signing the lease on the house in Crown Hill, sobbing with rage, drove through a red light, swerved to avoid a collision, and crashed her car against a telephone pole. From the hospital bed she elicited quite a nice divorce settlement from a Roger overcome with guilt.

She maneuvered herself into a comfortable position with Callie on the couch. Tears rolled down her cheeks. Callie woke up, put her paw on Libby's arm, and went back to sleep.

Chapter Two

Kay poses behind a hydrangea, Chalice communes with a snake, a squirrel takes communion, and Libby meets her past

On Saturday morning April sat admiring her handiwork in her garden. She had distributed the mulch piles around the fruit trees, roses, and newly planted kale and mustard. Her winter pansies greeted visitors with an invitation to follow them around the house to the patio, where she and Bob sat drinking coffee surrounded by pots of geraniums. It was still warm enough for the geraniums to spend their nights and for the Marches to spend their mornings out of doors. This particular Saturday was in fact an exceptionally warm morning for the last day of August.

Rambles sniffed the mulch under the Cherry Bomb, padded over to April, and jumped onto the front section of the *New York Times,* causing her to spill coffee.

"Oh, Rambles, get down."

Rambles cocked his head reproachfully.

"Oh, all right. Here."

She set aside the paper and waited while Rambles did a few turns on her lap before committing himself to a slumber position. April attempted to get comfortable, holding her newspaper higher and reaching across her body with her left hand to pick up her coffee mug. Rambles purred.

The sound of a motor came from around the corner. A white Porsche dove into the parking strip outside the March house, scattering gravel, scudding to a halt. A head as white as the car emerged from the driver's side.

"Are you expecting Gwen?" Bob asked.

"She's going to photograph Kay."

Cautiously: "Doing what?"

"Posing naked behind the hydrangea. She'll be Eve in her old age."

"Are all your pictures going to be of naked women?"

"Not all of them. Why? Did you want to pose naked?"

"No."

"You're missing an important aspect of this photo. It isn't just Kay. It's my hydrangea."

April's late blooming hydrangea was stunning. It brought to her mind aubergine and red grapes with turns of blackberry and plum. It was all the late summer fruits. It was the color of royalty. It was the color of April's pride.

"Do I need to leave home?"

"I don't think she'd want you two feet away with a handful of singles, but Kay's not going to care if you're around."

"Halloo." Gwen Pennant tottered down the walk on her stilettos, her white harem pants ballooning below a black tank top and her long gold pendant earrings tinkling in the morning breeze. She carried a camera in one hand and a laptop in the other. "Where am I working? I need a table."

Rambles jumped off April and disappeared into the house.

Kay's car pulled into the parking strip. April went to meet her. A flip-flop footed bare leg emerged from the driver's side. Kay heaved the rest of her body out. She was in a quilted green and yellow zip-up bathrobe. April grinned.

"There was no point in getting dressed. But is my hair okay?"

"We'll fix it." April fluffed Kay's hair as she followed her through the gate and down the side yard, where Bob was setting up a card table. "Don't worry. Bob won't be anywhere near."

"Not worried about Bob but..." Kay waved her arm toward the street, where dog-walkers were pretending their dogs were peeing for longer than it took their dogs to pee. "Do you have a screen of some kind?"

Bob set up an old privacy screen that April had been trying for years to sell in her annual garage sale. He saluted the group of women, who were looking at him expectantly. "I'll be inside."

April kissed him. "We won't be long. Thanks."

Gwen circled the hydrangea and looked at the sky. "We've got some really nice light. We should do this right away. Let's figure out where you're going to be."

Still in her robe, Kay took up poses standing behind the hydrangea, then sitting on a garden bench.

Gwen murmured as she paced in front of the hydrangea. "No, the light's not right there. Try moving two inches to the left. More. Now put your arm out to take that branch, no, forget that. OK, I think that's good. Get naked before the sun moves."

Kay unzipped her robe and kicked off her flip-flops. April gathered them and stood to the side, watching Kay with admiration. Gwen clicked away, moving the camera by inches after each shot.

"OK, I think that's all I can do now. Let me get these into Photoshop and we'll see what we've got."

April helped Kay with her robe. "I bet you're chilled."

"Not a bit. I feel hot, actually. That was fun!"

The three women were sitting at the garden table looking at photos on Gwen's laptop when Marvin, the Min Pin sans leather coat, came trotting down the walk. Behind him, Corinne, carrying a full garbage bag, chewed a wad of gum. Still in green tights, she was without her army jacket and orange crocheted scarf.

"Hey, Corinne. Out for your morning constitutional?"

"Yeah. I wanted to take these to the church but someone's changed the code on the side door."

"What are they?" April asked.

Corinne pulled out a series of odd-shaped and various-sized stuffed fabric lumps. As a species they appeared to be pillows, festooned with the sort of tackle box embellishments that Corinne favored on her clothes and on Marvin's leather coat.

"What are they?" April asked again.

"I thought they could be kneelers."

"Corinne, you don't kneel at your church."

"Well, then back pillows."

"Or butt pillows for our members who have sticks up their butt," Kay volunteered. "I bet it was Esme who changed the code."

As April was examining these extraordinary artifacts, a white Subaru Legacy came down the street, slowing in front of April's house. Eyes under a baseball cap searched April's yard. The car shot ahead.

"Was that Kimberly?" April asked.

Kay prodded a triangular-shaped lump, blue paisley on one side, red plaid on the other, pinned in several places and sporting an old army medal. "Yeah. Looks like she's on her way up to Tulalip."

"Tulalip. What for?"

"She goes to the casino. She thinks nobody knows."

"Are you kidding? And in a baseball cap?"

"She wears that cap when she goes up there," Corinne confirmed. "She took me once."

Minutes later Kimberly came around the corner of the house, baseball cap gone and her hair fluffed higher than usual.

"Hello, there," she said brightly. "I was in the neighborhood and saw the group of you. I thought, oh, there's always something fun going on at April's! What are you up to?"

April frowned. She couldn't recall Kimberly ever actually being here.

"Taking nudie photos," Kay said. "You should pose, Kimberly."

"I'll go make coffee," April said. She halted. This was going to be too good to miss.

Gwen turned the computer around. "Here we go," she said. "What do you think of this one?"

The photo on the computer showed seventy-eight-year-old Kay partially hidden by the hydrangea. There was cleavage. There was the suggestion of a nipple amongst the purple blossoms. Through some broken branches in the lower half of the bush, there flowered a mound of lush purple where another type of mound would otherwise be. And finally there was a foot and an ankle casually resting in the earth to the side of the bush. Gwen had played with the light so the green of the garden behind Kay made her body pop into view behind the dark vibrancy of the hydrangea.

Kimberly gasped, "Oh, my."

Kay beamed. "I love it," she said. "How do you do that, Gwen? I look so sexy."

"This isn't for your calendar," Kimberly said in an ominous tone.

"Yes, it is," April said. "Now, who wants coffee?"

Kimberly looked from April to Kay to Gwen to Corinne, who was stuffing pillow lumps into her garbage bag. "You cannot associate a calendar of nude photographs with Crown Hill Community Church. You cannot."

"They aren't all going to be nude," Kay said. "We were thinking of doing one up at the Tulalip casino using an offering plate. But everyone would be fully clothed."

Kimberly bit her lower lip. She laughed nervously. "You know this can't happen. We'll need to discuss this in council."

"That was mean," April said when Kimberly had stumbled down the walk and rounded the corner.

"Oh, she'll get over it. And it will keep Victor out of your garden because she'll report to him that I'm in charge."

Chalice perched on a stool in her kitchen between an open cupboard and the kitchen table. A garbage pail and a recycling container gaped beside her. A battalion of supplement bottles had commandeered the table, pushing aside a plate with crumbs from yesterday's cake and the remains of a small child's lunch: a miniature car upended in half a glass of milk and a piece of bread stamped flat.

Chalice reviewed the troops: twenty-three pill containers, eight tincture bottles, seven jars of liquids, and two large cans labelled "Spiritus-2" and "Mystifix-87." Having purged the house of sugar, she was now sorting and purging her supplements, emptying their contents into the garbage, and dropping the containers into the recycling.

The phone rang. Chalice picked up and listened. She rummaged for a pen and responded, "OK, I'll cut back on the B-complex and up the Mystifix-87. Yes, I know, no soy."

The small child whose lunch was now a demolition site had taken a short "rest," in which he had kept his presence known to his parents in the form of whines. After half an hour, his father had outfitted him with knee pads, elbow pads, gloves, and a bike helmet.

"Maybe he'll sleep later," Kirk said as he ushered Chase out the door.

"Bye, Chasie," Chalice said absently. She stared at a bottle of bile acid salts and tried to remember when she had last used them and for what reason. "Love, love, love, love, love."

At last the house was quiet. Chalice summarily finished her sorting. She took a deep breath and invited peace to enter her. She had things to do that required quiet. She made a motion as though to pull off her own head and launch it into the universe. It was something she did when she wanted to clear her psychic space.

She was protective of her psychic space. She sensed things. She saw auras. She might have gone Wiccan or become a placard-displaying psychic or a new age spiritualist. She might have chosen any number of filters through which to push her sensitivities, but she had chosen a kind of eclecticism amounting to a system of checks and balances. What truly kept Chalice from launching her entire being into the universe was music.

She was a talented musician and Crown Hill Comm was lucky to have her, though few of them knew it, certainly not Victor. A competent pianist and conductor, she had a mezzo-soprano voice that matched the richness of the instrument of her heart: the cello. Her highest hopes for a career in music had stalled when she became pregnant with Chase. Theoretically she had wanted a child. Postpartum depression had given way to a rocky five years in which she had tried to be the mother she felt she was expected to be while keeping her musical skills alive at the same time.

Chalice sat down in the corner of the dining room where her cello lived with a childproof fence around it. She sat with her arms around her instrument for a minute or two and breathed. Then she slowly began to play the prelude from the second Bach cello suite. She played it a second time a little faster.

She set the cello aside. Behind a cabinet that housed six-year-old unused wedding gifts — the Regift Cabinet — her fingers unhooked a key with which she unlocked a deep drawer.

Out of the drawer she carefully lifted something shrouded in a midnight-blue velvet cloth. She set it on the table and reverently removed the cloth. Her arms embraced a wreath-like pottery creation of deep greens, blues, and purples that she had made at a Do It Yourself pottery studio: a snake, its undulating body circling round to where the tail of the snake disappeared inside its mouth.

The Ouroboros.

She breathed in. She breathed out.

It was a ritual she performed often in these weeks leading up to the first meeting of her spirituality group. She still had only a nascent vision for this gathering but she believed the Ouroboros would speak to her eventually. Maybe lay out a flow of ideas that would coalesce into a program. She wanted to be prepared for the messiness of the human condition, but not too prepared. One needed to leave room for the serendipitous, for synchronicity, for the gods and goddesses to play, for something unexpected to pierce the veil between the worlds.

The doorbell interrupted her meditation. She considered not answering it. It would be so lovely to sit here quietly until Kirk and Chase returned. It rang again. She got up.

She should have taken a leaf from April's garden and hidden. It was Victor at the door, all smiles and solicitousness.

"Chalice," he said. "I hope I'm not disturbing you."

"I'm in the middle of something," she said flatly.

"This will just take a minute." He looked as though he expected an invitation inside.

She was usually compliant with Victor but she craved solitude. "What?"

"Can I come in for just a minute?"

"I'm in the middle of something."

Victor blinked. "You were right about the music festival. We should set our sights on Christmas."

Chalice waited.

"Also…Kim and I got your invitation. Your little spirituality group idea seems to be happening quickly."

Chalice narrowed her eyes.

"I wondered if there was some way I could help you. You're probably new at these things."

"Thank you, Victor. I'll let you know if I need any help."

"You and Jeff and I need to get together and plan for Christmas," he said as Chalice firmly shut the door.

"*Little* spirituality group," she muttered. "That was a mistake."

Sunday morning, Kimberly, Victor, and Jeff all arrived at the church at the same time but in three different cars. Talking Heads blared out of Jeff's Volvo. Loud talking rumbled from Victor's Cadillac. Kimberly's Subaru was silent. She had lost a lot of money at Tulalip the day before and didn't want to listen to Victor's inspirational tapes or be married to him. She chewed at her lip.

She watched Jeff get out of his car, yawn, and balance his coffee mug on his music. He ambled across the parking lot to where she was now picking at her lips with her fingers and opened her car door for her. As they walked to the church, Jeff passed Kimberly a tissue.

"Your lip is bleeding," he said.

She would have liked to cry except that Kimberly never cried.

Jeff unlocked the church door and they entered together while Victor continued to sit in his car, presumably being inspired.

The semidark foyer was warm with the fragrant softness of April's white and pink stocks. In the front of the sanctuary, she had arranged dahlias under the pulpit. Tall sunflowers stood in the sea of green by the piano. A long swathe had been rerouted to obscure the hole made by the church's mystery rodent. Kay and her son Jerry had evidently swept through, because there was a goddess-y looking statue in the curve of the grand piano, surrounded by laurel leaves and more sunflowers. Kimberly and Jeff took it in together. Jeff chuckled. Kimberly sighed.

A soft light illuminated the communion table. Kimberly turned on an overhead light, revealing a display as disheveled as her husband's mind. She came slowly down the aisle, staring in confusion as it took on the look of a breakfast table after everyone had left to brush their teeth. The loaf of bread — the body of Christ — that Victor liked to hold dramatically above his head and ceremoniously break apart was already in several pieces. The communion cloth hung to the floor, bringing the chalice of wine — the blood of Christ — precariously close to the edge of the table.

Crumbs dribbled onto the floor and trailed to the front pew, where sat the morning's first worshipper, a brown squirrel in a pile of lumpy pillows, chewing rapturously on a hunk of blessed bread. It came out of its ecstasy when Kimberly reached the front of the church. Both beings froze, one alert, the other horrified. They had achieved a kind of détente, but Jeff's arrival and subsequent full-throated laugh shot the squirrel into a parabola toward its Sunday dinner and then back to disappear under the pews.

"I guess our first congregant has arrived," Jeff said.

The sanctuary door opened and Brianna's mother, Wanda, came thumping down the aisle in her beige Naturalizer shoes, her Coach bag banging against her.

"What *happened* here?" Wanda spread her hands from the communion table to the pew with its riot of crumbs and back again. The Coach rocked back and forth on her arm.

Jeff turned on the organ. He played the death march from *Saul* with the sixteen-foot Double Diapason.

"You think this is funny?" Wanda demanded.

"Not now that you're here."

"Jeff," Kimberly said repressively. She needed a crisis like this to pull her into focus. She became The Minister's Wife again. She rescued the wine chalice from its uncertain future and picked up the bread tray.

"We'll have to get rid of this. Wanda, could you wipe all these crumbs onto the tray and then go get the vacuum? I'll have to see what's in the freezer."

"The freezer? But the bread, it's *consecrated,* isn't it? You can't just fill in with common bread." Wanda waved her wrists. Her purse banged against Kimberly. "Do we *have* a spare loaf? Maybe for the *symbolism,* you could just this once use something *common,* or well you know what I mean, but — "

"Wanda, *Wanda*! It's okay."

Kimberly put her hand on Wanda's arm, preventing the purse from hitting her one more time. She calculated the mess around the communion table. "It'll be fine. Look, I'll do this. You go get the small vacuum in the vestry."

Wanda bustled off. Jeff came forward with the waste can he kept by the organ. It had several weeks' worth of Panda black licorice wrappers in it.

"Did Danny trap for squirrels?" he asked.

"He had to rent a squirrel trap. He set it yesterday." Kimberly dropped the largest hunks of bread in the waste can. "Thanks, Jeff."

"Well, I don't know. Can you just *plop* consecrated bread in a *common* waste can?"

"Jeff, you do know that Wanda is on the board that hires and fires?"

"Yes, I'm frightened." Jeff took the can over to the pew where the squirrel had celebrated the Eucharist. "What a feast he had. Cute little guy."

Wanda came panting around the corner with the vacuum cleaner, its cord unraveling. Her Coach banged against the pulpit and almost knocked over the vase of dahlias and ferns. She thunked everything onto the floor and began pulling the electrical cord through the straps of her bag.

"Do you want some help, Wanda? I could hold your purse, for instance." Jeff drained his cappuccino.

"Jeff," Kimberly said smoothly. "Go get the loaf in the freezer. Put it in the microwave. Here, Wanda, let me help you."

Kimberly untangled the mess of vacuum cleaner cord from Wanda's purse straps and plugged it into the outlet at the base of the pulpit.

"Let's shake out the cloth first," she said. "Help me move these things. There's no need to rush; we have plenty of time."

The clock on the back wall said nine-thirty. It was purposely set fifteen minutes fast in hopes that Victor in full flow would occasionally end on time.

Wanda, yanking flowers and bowls off the table, looked ready to face down armies of invading squirrels. Water spilled out of the vase she was holding. She sank down in a lump and a sob on the front pew. "Oh, this day!" she wailed.

"What's this day been doing to you, Wanda?" Kimberly asked. She didn't want to know nor did she care but The Minister's Wife asks. She gathered up the communion cloth and shook it into the waste can.

"Brianna. She came home last night reeking of opium and tattoos. This morning, well, you should see what she thought she was coming to church in. I told her to clean her face and change and be up here to help with the coffee in ten minutes. You watch. She'll come in late and she'll have even more make-up on. When does choir start?"

Kimberly had arranged the chalice, bread plate, and flowers during this recital. She'd heard it before, except for the opium, so all she said was, "The choir?"

"She's easier to manage on Sunday when there's choir."

"Wanda, why don't you sit in the vestry and look over the order of service and the extra announcements for this morning? Brianna is seventeen. You can't really manage her."

She handed Wanda her black bag and gave her a little hug and a push toward the vestry.

Jeff maneuvered the vacuum over the carpet. "I'll do this," he said. "Go help Victor get his boas on."

Since Kimberly and Victor weren't actually on speaking terms that morning, Kimberly thought her time would be better spent coping with Wanda, who was to be that morning's worship leader. That Brianna would be in the congregation unsupervised wasn't going to help her mother's concentration. She went into the vestry where Wanda sat at the table, still stacked with dusty music from Friday's archaeological dig.

Kimberly sat down with Wanda and together they looked over the order of service. Victor had marked all the worship leader parts with a highlighter, with underlines, with exclamation points, and sometimes with all three. How many times had Kimberly told Victor that this was insulting, not to mention unnecessary?

The announcement that choir rehearsals began the Thursday after Labor Day was highlighted. The date for laying out the labyrinth was highlighted and underlined twice. It was the Saturday two weeks after Labor Day. Kimberly frowned. When had *that* been decided? As far as she could tell, Victor had made no actual plans or consulted anyone about how to create a labyrinth. Prayers were asked for Fred Johansen II, who was in the hospital after a hernia operation (neither highlighted nor underlined).

Corinne wanted everyone to know they could take their cats and dogs to the QFC parking lot on 130th for cheap rabies shots. Exclamation point. Wanda asked why she was obliged to make that announcement. Kimberly said that Corinne had to be humored or she was likely to volunteer the announcement when she felt a lull in the service.

Kimberly crossed out an announcement about a spirituality group called Ouroboros at the end of September. She opened a lavender folder that was lying on the table. "What's this?"

Kimberly looked for a long time at the photo of Chalice naked behind some music with flames of hell rising behind her. My God, what was happening? Had some pod women risen up from beneath the earth and invaded Crown Hill Comm while she was choosing floor tiles and wall paint for the new wing?

"What is it?" asked Wanda.

"Nothing." Kimberly scooped up the lavender folder and marched out.

Kimberly sat through the morning's sermon, which appeared to be about the persistence of rodents, chewing her lip. There were four women involved in this calendar business. So far. Chalice, April, Gwen, and Kay.

Chalice wasn't at the service. She only came when the choir was singing. Kimberly didn't know Chalice's husband Kirk; he was always preoccupied with that child of theirs. April had a kind of immunity from prosecution because she wasn't a church member. Bob couldn't be leaned on because he and April had, as Kimberly saw it, a feminist marriage. Gwen was easily distracted by anything visual and tended to go on and on about the patterns she saw. She was also immune to the kind of morality that Kimberly wanted to demonstrate. Kay would be the one to confront. Wait. Confront was the wrong approach to Kay. She would dig in deeper. Kimberly would have to think carefully about this. Her lip began to bleed again.

During the benediction, Brianna Carpenter popped a grape gum bubble that could be detected by three of the five human senses and all age groups in the sanctuary. Finally the service was mercifully over. The Minister's Wife slipped out the door and got in her car. A block from the church she pulled a Mariners baseball cap out of the glove box and put it on.

Libby maneuvered herself down the few steps from her house to the street, Callie doing ecstatic circles around Libby's crutches and trapping her in the leash. She moved carefully down the uneven street edges of Crown Hill. Her dog's enthusiasm calmed into a proud prance but revved up again when they got to April's front gate. Callie had been in this yard before; there was plenty to interest her.

Libby closed the gate behind them and let out the leash. Rambles, curled up in the birdbath that April had cleaned but not yet filled, looked disapprovingly at the dog and then went back to sleep. Libby was breathing in a late red rose when April came around the corner of the house.

"Hey, there you are! I was just stirring the compost and I'm ready for a break. Let me go wash my hands. Have a seat. Coffee?"

As Libby waited under April's big patio umbrella, an old Cadillac pulled up to the church across the street. A man got out. Libby watched him idly. He had a bit of a belly but not much of a butt. He gestured as though to brush back more hair than he currently possessed. A memory stirred in Libby.

April came out, her breasts a little lower than when she went in, with a French press in one hand, two mugs in another.

"What's the name of your pastor?"

"First of all, he's not my pastor. But if you mean the pastor of the church across the street, his name is Victor."

"Is that him?"

April looked up. Victor was inspecting his face in the Cadillac's side-view mirror. "Yep, that's him."

Libby swallowed. "Good God."

"I doubt anyone has ever said that about Victor!" laughed April. She pushed the plunger on the French press.

"No, I mean, well, you remember I told you I knew a divinity student at Berkeley?"

"Knew in the Biblical sense. I remember." April poured two mugs of coffee.

"His name was Victor." Libby stared backward into her past.

"You're not thinking this is the same Victor?" April pushed a mug across the table.

"I don't know. The Victor I knew had a big mop of hair that he used to push back in a certain way — the way the man across the street did just now, only he doesn't have as much hair. But there was something I haven't told you. This divinity student I knew...after we slept together and he disappeared, I found out I was pregnant."

April sat down with a thump.

"Abortion had only been legal for a few years. I grew up in a conservative religious family. I don't know if you remember but back then the conservatives didn't have a problem with abortion — well, Catholics did but not the Protestants. My parents would have been okay with it. What they weren't okay with was what they called 'sex out of wedlock.' It was all moot, though, because I didn't tell them about any of it."

"You had an abortion?"

"In Berkeley."

At that moment, the Victor in question appeared, sauntering down the sidewalk alongside the house. April reached for a sun visor hanging off a patio chair and pushed it across the table. "Here. Put this on."

Libby had the advantage — just barely — in what was about to occur, but she suddenly felt woozy. She put on the sun visor.

By the time Victor arrived at the patio table, Libby knew it was the same man she had known twenty-five years ago. His gait sketched in the final detail. He smiled expansively at the two women.

"Good morning, ladies! April, is Bob around?"

"He's in the house somewhere."

Victor looked at Libby. "Hello, I'm Victor. Have we met?"

Libby had had enough drama in her recent life to last her the rest of it but the scene now playing was unrelenting in its demands. "I'm Libby," she said.

Victor stared. "Libby."

"We knew each other at Berkeley."

"Yes, we did! Well, how have you…" His face blanched. "It's been a long time."

"Yes."

"How have you been?"

Libby looked at him with distaste. She didn't care that she was conflating him with her ex-husband. "April and I were talking about abortions," she said dispassionately.

The smile on Victor's face froze. April inched her chair a little closer, but what Libby needed was a toilet, whether to shit or to throw up, she couldn't quite tell. She felt sick but she still had control of the scene.

"April," she said. "I'm going to the bathroom. Can you help me?"

Bob came through the sunroom door. "Here, let me," he said to Libby.

He took her elbow, collected her crutches, and helped her into the house.

"Can you manage all right? This bathroom is small, a powder room, really. Maybe you'd rather use mine and April's? It's wider."

"This is fine," Libby whispered. "Thank you."

Libby didn't throw up. She didn't shit. She sat on the edge of the toilet lid until her stomach felt calmer. She thought that a man like Bob March made it hard to hate all men.

When she came out of the powder room, Callie was lying on the floor in the pantry off the kitchen, her head on her paws. She thumped her tail three times before she got joyously up and pushed her nose against Libby's thigh. In the kitchen, Rambles disapproved from the top of the refrigerator. April plunged a second pot of coffee. Bob hovered.

"He's gone," April said immediately. "I've made more coffee."

Libby looked at Bob. "Did April fill you in?"

"That you knew Victor in college?"

"That he knocked me up and disappeared, leaving me pregnant."

Bob looked at his wife. "She didn't mention that."

"And now I live down the street from his church."

"Let's go back outside. Honey, come with us. Stay at least until the man-bashing begins," April said.

Bob smiled wryly and rinsed out a mug.

The three sat under the patio umbrella. Libby sensed that April was primed for a good gossip and Bob was poised to flee if necessary. There was a long silence.

"What were you doing at Berkeley?" Bob finally asked.

"Trying to figure out what I wanted to do. Art. Women's Studies." Libby stared ahead of her. "Victor wasn't any great passion but he was my first. I was naïve, he was older, blah, blah, blah, although he wasn't experienced at all or nuanced or even particularly sensitive."

"He married someone named Kimberly."

"Kimberly. Not Kimberly Kendrick?"

April looked at Bob. "Is that her birth name? Kendrick?"

"I think so."

"There was a Kimberly Kendrick in the Berkeley church. I saw her once or twice at the women's clinic. She clearly wanted me to think she was there for a checkup but the gossip went round later that she had gotten an abortion and then gone back home to Phoenix."

"Victor interned in Phoenix," Bob said.

"Whoa, back up! Kimberly the Conservative had an abortion?" April looked gleeful.

"April," Bob said repressively. "We don't know if we're even talking about the same person. Don't gloat."

"I'm not gloating. Well, maybe just a little. OK, a lot. It's just that Kimberly Cummings is so sanctimonious toward other people's behavior."

"So was Kimberly Kendrick."

"Do you think she would recognize you?"

"I don't know. Maybe." Libby looked at the garden. She suddenly wanted to change the subject. "You said something about putting in a labyrinth."

"Yeah, at the church," Bob said.

"No, here. April, didn't you say you wanted to build a labyrinth here in your garden?"

"April?" Bob looked at his wife.

"It was just an idea."

"An idea to rattle Victor."

"That's what Brianna said," Libby remembered. "Only I think the phrase 'fuck you' was used."

"I hereby go on record saying I think it's a bad idea," said Bob.

"Oh, Bob, listen." April put her hand on his arm. "Victor isn't going to build that labyrinth. It's one of his big ideas, but he hasn't a clue what's involved. No one has the time or energy to do the work and the church can't afford to hire anyone. He should just get a roll-up plastic labyrinth or paint one on the floor of his new wing and call it a day."

"You could do something magnificent in your yard." Libby stood up, steadied herself against the patio table, and surveyed the property. "You could create a labyrinth that winds though the plants and trees and with little hermes and places to sit."

"Hermes?"

"You know, little markers."

"I could do a lot of the physical work myself, and I bet I could corral some of my students to help. Be right back. I'm getting a pen and paper."

Libby and Bob looked at each other.

"Your wife is a force majeure."

"She is at that."

"Do you really think this is a bad idea?"

"If it has to do with the garden, April knows what she's doing. Do you feel any better?"

"Getting there."

Chapter Three

Kimberly does an inspection, and the Music Committee meets

By the Tuesday after Labor Day, Kimberly and Victor were behaving like nodding acquaintances.

"Have they caught the squirrel?"

"I don't know."

Kimberly drove to the church and went through the side door to the office where Esme ruled her little kingdom of inefficiency.

"Have you heard from Danny?"

Esme stopped typing. She undid her stringy hair and twisted it back up on her head. She looked at Kimberly absently. "Danny?"

"Danny. He set the squirrel trap on Saturday."

"Well, actually he hasn't set it yet. He couldn't figure out how to use it so he took it back to wherever he got it to ask them. He's going to set it sometime this week."

"This week! We should have gotten that squirrel out five days ago." Kimberly could see an email on the computer. "What are you working on?"

"I just finished." Esme closed the email program. FreeCell Solitaire appeared. She closed the laptop. "What do you need?"

"If you would just stay on top of Danny and the squirrel." Long sigh. "Victor meets with the music committee this afternoon and he needs a block of time to finish a draft of Sunday's sermon for me to edit."

Kimberly went into the vestry, which reminded her of the lavender folder with the nudie picture — she didn't know quite how to cope with the calendar uprising yet. She went through the sanctuary and into Victor's office. Her husband's desk looked like a salvage yard. Pens and a rubber-band ball had been shoved aside to make space for his laptop, which was still open, still on, and raised on one side by a legal pad. Choir music for a song called "There Shall a Star Come out of Jacob" sat on the keyboard. A stack of printouts from web pages sat next to it. A pile of manila folders hung precariously off one edge, weighed down by books with sticky notes flapping in all directions. A stack of papers and envelopes rose from the In tray.

The Out tray had a single envelope in it, addressed to Sharper Image. Kimberly held it up to the light. There was a check inside. The Sharper Image catalog was open to wine paraphernalia and Victor had highlighted, underlined, and put an exclamation point next to an expensive bottle opener.

She sat at the desk. Her feet bumped something heavy underneath it. She looked down. A box. She pushed it with her foot. It didn't budge. She pushed back the chair, moved "There Shall a Star Come out of Jacob" off the computer keyboard, and pulled the laptop onto her lap. She clicked on Internet History and saw that Victor had been looking at websites having to do with the old Berkeley church where they had met. She frowned. Was that sweet or ominous?

She continued down the Internet History list. Servanthood. Kimberly raised her eyebrows. She thought she had schooled him sufficiently that a man preaching about servanthood to a congregation that included women was a dicey business. Still, everyone was tired of the Stewardship angle now that two sermons a month were touching on the need to raise money. This was a church in which fund-raisers mostly involved the usual congregants passing the same money back and forth at book, bake, and rummage sales. Having a good time but not really raising any new funds.

She put the computer back and thumbed through the stack of website printouts. Victor had highlighted whole pages of "Goals and Visions for the Church Musician" from a website called Joyful Noise. He had highlighted and underlined bullet points and added lots of exclamation points.

The last sheet in the stack was a photo of a labyrinth.

Kimberly picked up the legal pad. Victor had written the names Chalice and Jeff and had begun a vague accounting of their separate duties. Kimberly put everything back where it had been, not that Victor would notice one way or the other.

She got down on her hands and knees and pulled the heavy box toward her. Someone had written "COMMUNION!" on the lid. She lifted bottles of wine one by one to read their labels. Cabernet Sauvignon, Syrah, Malbec, Pinot Noir. Expensive wine. Much of it foreign. Not the table wine they used for Communion. And they wouldn't need this much Communion wine in a year.

She left the study, chewing her lip, and turned into the new wing. Four carpeted rooms could be used as classrooms or sleeping quarters. Kimberly had chosen the colors for each of the rooms: Butter Cream, Am I Blue?, Lime Daiquiri, and Watermelon Pickle. The two bathrooms at either end of the suite of rooms had been tiled Spore Green and Mutiny Blue. The far end of the wing opened onto a large hexagon-shaped room with a deep red carpet (Claret Red), a domed ceiling, a stage at one end, and a kitchen at the other.

Kimberly's eyes roamed the room. She took in the smartness of the kitchen. She appreciated how efficiently the space had been laid out. Of course it had been to her specifications.

Knobs under the stage suggested drawers or cupboards. Kimberly hadn't remembered there would be storage space there. Good to know. She opened one of the cupboards to find another box labeled COMMUNION! Kimberly pulled out more bottles. Gewurztraminer, Semillon, Pinot Grigio. Expensive, white, definitely *not*-for-communion wine.

Kimberly sat back on her heels and took a breath. Her lip was bleeding. The rooms were filled with the smell of newness but were empty of anything a person could sit on, sleep on, wash with, cook with, or spoon into one's mouth. Except this. And what was this for? Catching fruit flies? Victor had supposedly organized a committee to take care of furnishings. As far as Kimberly could tell, the wing's single furnishing was to be a wine bottle opener and two dozen bottles of not-for-communion wine.

Chalice entered the vestry and summarily disposed of the rest of the old choir music. There were two cabinet drawers she hadn't gone through but she had seen enough. In a dozen trips she lugged the music to the recycle bin. She was still outside and brushing the dust off her clothes when Jeff arrived with a cardboard coffee tray. In two of the compartments were large drinks. A bag of trail mix covered the rest of the tray.

"Iced herb tea for you, milady," he said. "Chalice, you know this meeting with Victor doesn't mean anything. It's just a chance for him to blather on about whatever idea he's recently picked up. You and I will go on as usual."

Chalice hadn't seen Victor since she closed the door in his face. "Thank you, Jeff," she said gratefully. "Shall we go?"

"Into the fray."

When they entered the pastor's study, Victor gave the impression of an industrious someone with important things on his mind. Chalice sat, uncomfortable but alert. Jeff opened the bag of trail mix and pushed it toward her. He sat back, took a slow draught of his drink, and waited.

Victor handed each of them a thick web printout of "Goals and Visions for the Church Musician." Chalice paged doubtfully through hers. She skimmed one of the sheets:

> *Second Chronicles 5:13: The trumpeters and musicians played in union, praising and giving thanks to the LORD. They praised the LORD loudly and sang, "He is good, and his gracious love is eternal."*
> *Mission statement:*
> *The music ministry facilitates the overall mission of this church.*
> *Music should enhance the worship service.*
> *Music should edify and inspire.*

"Chalice," said Victor, "I would like to coordinate the choir music with the sermons so that we support and complement each other."

Chalice read the line in "Goals and Visions for the Church Musician" even as Victor was reciting it.

Chalice looked at Jeff, who shook his head a fraction of an inch from left to right. He was clearly trying not to smile. Chalice relaxed a little and thought about her choir.

The soprano section consisted of two uncontrollable adolescents, Brianna being one of them, and a woman who did her nails during the sermon. The altos were strong primarily because of Gwen, the photographer who had taken the naked photo of Chalice and who had a rich, true alto. Wanda, Brianna's mother, could manage quite well once she learned the part and as long as Gwen was there. The tenors were Fred Johansen II, who was partially deaf, and Bob March. The basses were Monty McDougal and Susan Moore, who had declared she would only join the choir if she were allowed to sing bass even if she was a woman. Nicholas sang bass when he was home from college. Jeff could also sing bass from the piano or organ as needed.

Chalice was just grateful when a quorum showed up to rehearsal. But coordinating with Victor's sermons? Which tangent would he expect her to coordinate with?

Thinking about the choir put her in a stronger frame of mind. Music was her bailiwick and she knew her onions, as April might have put it. She knew what her choir could and couldn't do and most decidedly she knew Victor's sermons were pitiful. He couldn't be serious about these "Goals and Visions for the Church Musician." They didn't mean anything. And why quote Second Chronicles, for God's sake?

"Is this some sort of hazing?" she demanded.

Jeff snorted coffee down the front of his shirt.

"What do you mean?" Victor asked.

Jeff wiped his mouth. "Victor, it's a choir of adolescents, adults tired from a day of work, and deaf tenors. That Chalice gets what she does out of them is a small miracle. It's difficult enough finding music that works for them without adding extra complications."

Victor squirmed. "I take your point. But I think we always need to be trying to improve. Coordinating with sermons is something to aspire to."

"Yes, it is," said Jeff smoothly.

Chalice gaped. Jeff winked and pushed the trail mix closer to her. She laid aside her packet of "Goals and Visions for the Church Musician," sat back, and picked out some chocolate chips. That was when she spotted the stack of "There Shall a Star Come out of Jacob."

"What's that doing in here?" she asked.

Victor hesitated. "I thought I might put together an ensemble to sing it at the dedication of the labyrinth."

"*You* might put together an ensemble?" She stood up. "That's it. I'm done here." She adjusted her tunic and smoothed her skirt. Her long earrings rattled. "Excuse me."

Her sandals clicked indignantly as she marched through the sanctuary toward the vestry. Jeff caught up with her in the alley.

"Chalice," he said. "Don't take him seriously. He says so many things that in the end he never means anything. Think of his sermons."

"I try not to."

"Yeah, we all do. Look, I've known Victor a long time. Kimberly rules him. He can't bear to have any more women around him who are self-assured and good at what they do."

"Did you hear him usurp my role as choir director? And how is he going to put together an ensemble? What does he know about it?"

"Well, he was in that Auditioned Choir."

"Oh, please."

"Look, he's not going to put together an ensemble to sing at the labyrinth. You're right, he doesn't know how. He's not even going to build a labyrinth. Everyone knows that. Everyone except Victor."

"I didn't."

"OK, everyone except Victor and you. You haven't been here long enough."

Chapter Four

April lays a labyrinth, the altar is photographed, and Kimberly picks up a scent

On the Wednesday after Labor Day, Bob March was back in his classroom at Nathan Hale High School. April calculated that with the two weeks before her community college quarter began she could get a good start on her labyrinth. That morning she and Libby sat at the patio table, feeling safe from any more of Victor's surprise appearances, and sketched out a plan. Callie lay with her nose against the boot on Libby's leg. Rambles claimed a stump that under previous ownership had held a pot of Martha Washington geraniums. From this elevation he could keep an eye on the dog.

April paced the yard with a tape measure, calling out figures to Libby, who sat with pen and paper. Together they figured out that the labyrinth could accommodate nine circuits, although the outer circuits weren't strictly circles, as they had to veer around fruit trees and established sections of the garden. Libby suggested they station a hermes every place that the path diverged from an actual circle. Deviations from the expected path could offer sophisticated labyrinth walkers more complexity.

April marked the labyrinth center with a stake. She tied a rope, duct-taped at half the length of the first circle's diameter, and walked around the circle, dropping a trail of white flour until she had a circumference. She placed a few rocks along the floured area. She moved the duct tape farther down the rope and made the next circuit. By the third circuit she had run out of rocks.

She sat down with Libby.

"I don't know if I want to flour my whole yard until I have enough rocks to make the paths. That flour isn't going to stay put and we're going to need lots of rocks. This is where my classes can help. Maybe Bob's students."

"What about the church?"

"Oh, please. They are such an apathetic bunch."

"Here's one of them now, I think."

April looked up. "Oh, it's Kay. OK, she's an exception. You'll like her."

Kay came to a halt at the patio table and April made introductions.

"We're doing another photo at the church. Do you want to watch?"

April looked at Libby. "What do you think? Do you want to enter enemy territory?"

"Let's go," Libby said.

The three women entered the office from the side door and filed past Esme. Her mucous-colored hair had been wound into a knot at the top of her head, but strands were falling out because she was scratching her scalp with the chopstick that had held the knot. She glared at the intruders. Kay detoured into the water closet. Inside the church sanctuary, Gwen was fiddling with her camera and Madelaine McGuffin, the soprano who did her nails during the worship services, was fiddling with her skirt.

"Who is that dreadful woman in the office?" Libby asked.

"Oh, that's Esme, the church administrator. Ignore her."

"Here's the toilet paper," said Kay, coming in from the vestry.

"My God, what are you up to?" April laughed. She had been so preoccupied with the garden and Libby's revelations that she hadn't been thinking about the calendar. Left to her own imagination, Kay had come up with the most outrageous idea yet.

She had draped the altar with swathes of dark purple, indicating the spring liturgical season of Lent. She had strewn April's sunflowers—indicating autumn and the season of Ordinary Time—on the altar and the floor beneath. Madelaine stood at the altar and lit a candle. Her skirt was tucked up into her underwear and a square of toilet paper was stuck to one shoe. Gwen circled and clicked her camera.

"The caption is going to read 'Madelaine will be so embarrassed when she realizes she got the liturgical color wrong.'"

April snorted. "That's brilliant!"

"What will you do if that office person comes in?" Libby asked.

"She won't."

"Oops," murmured April. "We might have a bigger worry."

April sat down and smothered a smile as Kimberly came through the door of the vestry. She was stuffing cash in her purse and clearly had expected the sanctuary to be empty.

"Oh," she said brightly. "What's all... Madelaine, why are you...? Your dress... *Is that toilet paper and what are you doing with the altar?"* Her eyes took in Gwen and the camera. "Never mind, I know what you're doing and it ends here. If this calendar business goes any further, I, we...the church will sue."

April was horribly afraid she was going to get the giggles, but the look on Libby's face sobered her. Under lowered lashes, her friend was looking warily at Kimberly, who was suddenly whirling around the altar picking up sunflowers and straightening the altar cloth, lecturing as she moved.

"You are in the house of the Lord. This is the altar, the holiest part of the church." She snatched the purple cloth off the table. "It's not even the right color."

April forced herself to think about where she might get a lot more rocks for her labyrinth and willed herself to not look at Kay.

Kimberly's eyes swept the room. She blinked a few times at Libby, but her gaze ended up on Gwen. "Give me that film!" she demanded.

"It's digital," Gwen said.

"What does that *mean,* digital?" Kay asked of no one in particular.

April pushed her hand hard against her mouth.

"Get out," Kimberly ordered.

Kimberly sat in the church sanctuary after the defilers had left. Specters raced in a loop through her mind. She sat for a long time until the race became more of a parade and she could see the looming menaces one by one.

Victor. He was easily overwhelmed by the small fires in the church and then he became paralyzed. Kimberly looked around. This church should have been hers. With her teeth she peeled off skin from her lower lip.

Money. She had planned a trip to the casino that afternoon in hopes of winning back the petty cash she had lost during the summer. That was always the plan when she went to Tulalip. She was always trying to win back money.

Money. The wing wasn't ready to rent and the labyrinth meant to entice renters was just a photograph on Victor's desk. Nothing more. The loan was coming due and they were behind two payments.

That damn calendar and the unmanageable women behind it. Kay, April, and Gwen traipsed in front of her, images in her nightmare.

She closed her eyes.

Who was that other woman today? Something niggled Kimberly's brain. The software of a pastor's wife included rapid name and face recognition, but this woman's face was in the microfiche of Kimberly's brain, back before there was RAM. She opened her eyes. She was still clutching the purple cloth she had pulled off the altar. Older images floated up. Berkeley. A purple room. With pillows. A women's clinic. A face. That woman with the boot on her leg. Who was she?

Kimberly's heart, which had so recently grown quiet, started beating an alarm. She gathered her handbag and jacket. Still clutching the purple cloth, she left the church through Victor's study so she didn't have to walk past Esme. In her car she put on her Mariners cap and drove north.

By the time Kimberly was back home in her kitchen, sharpening knives and preparing to chop things, she was calmer. Coming back from Tulalip with $250 more than she went up with fluffed up her self-confidence. She had her phantoms in a row. When Victor came home she would lead with the calendar. No, wait. That was too incendiary. Money? God no. She needed something more neutral. They'd barely spoken in five days. Kimberly wasn't even sure where her husband was.

Suddenly he was in the kitchen.

"Where have you been?" she asked.

"The All-City Faith Conference board."

Kimberly was silent. She might need to recalibrate her approach. The Conference board always gave Victor a boost of self-confidence. He shone in meetings. He could expound his big ideas but never had to do anything more about them. People found Victor charming. Then he'd come home and expect Kimberly to find him charming. After nearly twenty-five years of marriage, Victor's charm was, to Kimberly, only intermittent.

"Do you remember at Berkeley, that woman you went out with for a while before you got the internship in Phoenix?" It was the least flammable thing on Kimberly's mind.

Victor turned on the kitchen tap. "No, not really." He scooped water into his mouth.

Kimberly got a glass. "Here."

"I don't know who she is."

"What?"

"Nothing. I mean I don't know what woman you're talking about." Victor gulped a glass of water. "I got a notice from the bank. We have to pay them by the end of January or, well, I don't know what will happen. We might lose the church. The petty cash has been disappearing."

Kimberly slowed down her chopping of the carrots. "What does that have to do with anything? You're not paying off the loan with petty cash."

She suddenly remembered the cases of wine she had found in the church. She put down the knife and looked at her husband. "What's happened to the money in the church account and the Conference's matching funds?"

"Nothing. But the petty cash does keep disappearing. Esme said you were at the church this afternoon."

"So?" Kimberly picked up the knife. The energy inside her felt mutinous. She tried to speak slowly, but she had the impression she was waving the knife and babbling. "You might lose your pastorate altogether if Kay and April follow through on their calendar. Did you know Gwen was involved? They were taking a vulgar photo at the altar this afternoon. Vulgar. I told them we would sue if they identify Crown Hill Comm in it."

"A pastor doesn't sue a congregant." Victor took the knife out of her hands. "Kimberly, what's going on with you?"

"What? Nothing. There was a woman there who looked like someone we knew in Berkeley. Well, you knew her better than I did. But she looked like her."

"Are you suggesting she took the petty cash?"

"What? No!"

"Then why are we talking about her?" Victor paused. "I have calls to make."

He took the knife with him. Kimberly heard his study door close. She wiped her hands on a towel and walked into the living room. There on the bottom shelf of a built-in bookcase was a box of photographs that had started in an envelope in Berkeley, filled a box in Phoenix, and moved into a bigger box in Seattle. Kimberly found the Berkeley envelope at the bottom of the box. One by one she studied the photos.

Chapter Five

Libby sorts her past, Chalice launches her head,

and the squirrel comes to choir practice

The next morning found Libby also looking at photographs. Brianna had collected a box of albums and stray photos and left it on the floor where she could peruse them from the comfort of the couch.

"OK, Callie, I am going to do this."

Callie thumped her tail.

Libby began going through the albums, pulling photos of her ex-husband out and tearing them in quarters. In one group photo her ex was standing next to the woman who had gone back east with him. She folded the photo and bit into the woman's face. She chewed it right off the page and spit it out. She rifled through the box until she found her official wedding photo in its lovely (plated) silver frame.

"I look so happy."

The dog raised an eyebrow and sighed.

She would have liked to smash the glass of the frame. Instead she removed the photo, set the glass on the coffee table, and knocked the frame into four pieces. She ripped her ex-husband out of the wedding portrait and bit a hole in his crotch.

The oldest of the albums was from her college days. She went through it slowly, removing photos of people she didn't remember or hadn't kept up with. She turned a page and there, like some artifact from another culture, was a photo of the old Berkeley gang eating ice cream cones in Ghirardelli Square. She was in the middle of the photo and there on the edge was Victor. She looked at the photo for a long time, not really seeing it, but thinking how odd it was to know that while she looked middle-aged now, she was, at the same time, the young, laughing woman in the photo.

In an hour's time she compressed three photo albums into one and collected a pile of debris at her feet. This had always been Libby's way of dealing with loss. After Victor left and after the abortion, she hadn't just put together a break-up box. She had practically razed her apartment, throwing things out that had nothing to do with the defunct relationship, things she liked and used and would come to regret tossing: a soup pot, a childhood teddy bear, earrings, shoes.

Now she sat back, tired from the effort of so much anger being forced through her fine-motor muscles. She picked up a well-worn book called *Breathing and Being*. She'd already read it three times.

"Now this again, Callie."

Callie blinked.

Libby fell asleep at chapter five of *Breathing and Being*. She woke up when Brianna, coming to walk Callie, rang her doorbell.

"I'll take her to Sandel Playground and give her a good run," Brianna said. "You okay?"

"Yeah. I was asleep."

"Is this why you wanted me to collect all that stuff?" Brianna indicated the pile of torn-up photos. She picked up the photo of Libby's ex with his crotch torn out and grinned. She put it under the frame glass on the coffee table.

"OK, let's go!" She collected the leash and hooked it on Callie's collar.

They were just out the door when Libby's phone rang: April.

"I have Wanda Carpenter over here. You know, Brianna's mother. She wants to meet you."

Libby looked out her corner window. Brianna and Callie were at the traffic circle. She watched them turn down 87th. Sandel Playground was a quarter mile away. Callie liked to sniff things.

"I have a window of about an hour."

"On our way."

Libby had just enough time to fluff her hair, shrug into her lopsided cardigan, and sweep the discarded photos into the box before she opened the door to April and Brianna's mother. She had Wanda's measure immediately: eager veneer, self-effacing to the point of self-erasing.

"Brianna doesn't know I'm here," Wanda said, twisting the handle of her Coach bag, the one that seemed grafted to her arm at all times. Her boxy body maintained its squares and angles even with knit pull-on pants and big shirts.

"She took the dog to the playground. They're usually gone an hour. Come in. Sit down."

"Wow, Brianna has put this place in order," April said.

"I don't know what I would have done without Brianna this past week."

Wanda went down on the couch like a felled tree. Her Coach bag loaded the edge of the frame glass on the coffee table and levered it up. It crashed down in three jagged pieces.

"Oh, dear." Wanda looked at the photo of the crotchless groom under the now broken glass. "Oh, my."

"It's fine. Makes it easier to dispose of when it's in pieces."

"I beg your pardon."

"Just leave it. Brianna can take care of it."

"Oh, you mean the glass. Yes... So Brianna *helps* you?"

"Pretty much anything I need."

"Yes, well, she doesn't do much at home." Wanda looked at the crotchless man again.

"When Nicholas comes home, his training doesn't always hold but I am so glad to see him, I fuss," said April.

"Home from college," Wanda looked up. "Yes, I remember when you first packed him off."

"Oh, yeah," April grinned. "It was a Sunday and we'd spent all morning getting him packed while the service was going on across the street. There was a lot of yelling back and forth until Esme came out and told us they could hear me cursing. She told me I needed to respect the ethos of the neighborhood. Odious woman."

"Now which one is Esme?" asked Libby.

"That woman in the office the other day," April said. "The one who glared at us."

"Are you part of a church yourself?" Wanda asked.

"No."

"Maybe you'll visit us sometime. Our pastor is lovely."

Libby kept her eyes on Wanda, who was again looking at the photo under the broken glass. "Is he?" she murmured.

"Yes, he's been so good to me and Brianna. And his wife is so capable and supportive. The two are perfect for our little congregation."

Libby's eyes flickered toward April and then back to Wanda. "Your daughter has been perfect as someone to help me."

"Isn't it interesting how different our experiences of the same person can be?" asked April.

Chalice was trying to commune with the Ouroboros in her dining room, but it almost seemed like the snake was having none of it. Every time she inhaled, the snake hissed back.

Breathe in.

"Victor called your Ouroboros meeting a 'little spirituality group.'"

Breathe in.

"Victor thinks he's capable of doing your job as choir director."

Breathe in.

"He's going to have an erection with that Mendelssohn piece."

Chalice smiled, remembering that April had suggested changing "and a scepter shall rise out of Israel." April was a good sort and everyone loved her husband. Both of them were so grounded, April almost literally. She was a woman of earth.

Chalice didn't know a lot of people in Seattle. They had moved to the city two years ago and last year had been her first year at Crown Hill Comm. Victor's seeming respect now felt to Chalice like condescension.

Breathe in.

"He's out to undermine you."

She wrapped her arms around the Ouroboros. The job was a paycheck not worth the insults. It's just that church musicians at least *got* a steady paycheck. It was never enough to live on, but, combined with teaching or a spouse's income, it helped carve out room to actually make music somewhere else. Except that she wasn't making music anyplace else except in the corner of her dining room where her cello lived.

She launched her head. Then she wrapped the pottery snake in its black velvet cloth and put it back in its special drawer.

She went into her bedroom and dug down in her underwear drawer, where she kept a stash of Valium. She sat down with her cello and played until the Valium kicked in and Chase's bus pulled up at the corner.

Chalice descended the steps of her front porch as Chase jumped off the last two steps of the bus and roared like a jet plane toward her. He dropped his lunch pail on her foot, did a noisy flight around the yard, and charged up the steps into the house. Chalice smiled bleakly as she followed him. Chalice tried to be a mom but she was not A Mom. Kirk was A Mom. For that Chalice was grateful. In the kitchen, Chase was sticking his finger into her Mystifix-87 and licking the stuff.

"Yuck!" Chase made a face.

Chalice grabbed the canister. Where had this child come from?

"Chasie," she said suddenly. "Let's go see April."

She handed Chase a granola bar and put a juice box in her pocket. They went out the back door and into the alley alongside the church, which brought them to the T intersection of Dibble Avenue and 88th, where the March home and garden sprawled on a lot and a half. Chase bounced alongside his mother as she walked up the slight incline.

"Boing, boing!" he shouted. "Boing, boing, boing, boing, boing!"

At the top of the alley they saw April, in heavy work gloves, on her parking strip, looking at two large piles of stones. Chalice grabbed Chase's hand as they crossed the street, Chase hopping on one foot.

April looked up.

"Are those your rocks?" he demanded, still hopping.

"They are." She fixed the child with a stare until he put both feet on the ground.

Chase grew quiet and Chalice wondered why she couldn't manage him like that. She could see his aura but she didn't know what to do with it.

"What are they for?"

"For a thing called a labyrinth."

"Has that finally gotten underway?" Chalice asked.

"Oh, you mean the church? No, this is for my garden."

"Really?" Chalice's mind twitched. She looked at April's magnificent yard just across the street from the neighborhood church. "Does this have anything to do with — no, Chase, leave those rocks alone."

"It's okay," April said. "Chase, you can touch the stones but only if you do what I say with them. Deal?"

Chase looked at her. He looked at his mother. Chalice just looked on.

"I'll give you some gloves and a wheelbarrow and I want you to wheel all these stones into the yard. Can you do that?"

Chase jumped up and down and nodded his head.

"OK, come on in, you two, while I get Chase his work tools."

Ten minutes later, the two women were seated on the patio watching Chase arduously push a child's wheelbarrow full of rocks. April had designated drop zones with handfuls of flour, which exploded on the ground in poofs. The boy had looked longingly at the bag of flour.

"Bob's quite interested in your Ouroboros thing," April said.

"He is?"

"Yeah, he's interested in ideas. I think he wanted to be part of a church because he felt like he never had much of a religious education."

"Does he think he's getting one across the street?"

"What goes on over there," April waved at the church. "That's what religion is. I think he wanted it to be something else."

"Something else? Something spiritual, you mean?"

"I guess. Spiritual. It's kind of a useless word to me. In my garden I feel like I'm part of everything that is. I don't know of a word for that."

"I feel that way when I'm playing my cello. But I have this other side. Mystical."

"Hard to be mystical with a preschooler in the house."

Chalice looked at her son making another trip with the wheelbarrow. She wanted to cry. She loved him, she did. But sometimes he felt like such an intrusion. "Motherhood. I wanted it to be something else. Kirk is the better mom."

"There's nothing wrong with that. Just because you're the woman, it doesn't mean you have to be the better parent — whatever that means — at every stage of your child's life. One day, Chase will be an age that you'll love. Or even if that doesn't happen, it doesn't mean something is wrong. That'll just be what happened."

"Was there an age when you didn't feel connected to Nicholas?"

"I didn't think about it like that. He was like one of my plants. I watered him and watched him grow. I enjoyed him and I'm happy with the son I have."

Chalice looked at April's hands, stained green from grass, with dirt under her nails.

"There's too much 'supposed to be this way' going around," April continued. "Things are what they are. I learned that from the garden. When something isn't flourishing, you either pull it out or move it."

Chalice took the juice box to her son, sitting on rocks looking like he wanted to throw a few. April followed with the flour and dribbled lines. She showed the child where she wanted stones spread out to create a path. Chase slurped the juice and handed the sticky box to his mother. He knelt in the grass and began lining up stones on the flour lines.

"So this labyrinth," Chalice said, picking up on an earlier thought. "Does it have anything to do with Victor's project?"

"God, no!"

"I wondered because I don't see where or how he's going to cram a labyrinth in over there."

"He's not. It's never going to happen."

"That's what Jeff says."

"I've never seen anyone less suited to the job he's in."

Chalice was thoughtful as she and Chase walked home down the alley. Kirk was home and Chalice gratefully handed their son over to him. She needed to ready herself for tonight's choir rehearsal.

At a quarter past seven, the mantel of the organ hosted five piles of music and a stack of choir folders. Chalice and Jeff were sitting on the chancel steps with cups of herb tea in their hands, waiting for the choir to arrive.

"We should put some gin in these," Jeff said.

"Do you suppose anyone is coming? Was it announced on Sunday?"

"It was announced. But you know what wasn't announced is your spirituality group. Are you still doing that?"

"It wasn't?" Chalice frowned. "I told Esme to put it in."

"She has no actual initiative of her own but she does tend to do as she's told until she's told otherwise."

"Who was worship leader?"

"Wanda."

Chalice's thoughts grew dark. God, it was hard to keep a light on sometimes. "Then it would have had to be Victor. He wanted to be part of it and I said no thank you."

"Kimberly was supervising Wanda on Sunday. She could have put the kibosh on it. Did you hear about the squirrel who came for communion?"

"Is this a joke?"

"Yes, but it really happened."

Chalice turned around to look for the hole the animal had chewed in the wall behind the choir stall, but it was still covered with green drapery.

"Haven't they caught that thing yet?"

Jeff described the hijack of the communion table but Chalice's mind was elsewhere. She felt sabotaged: the music, her spirituality group. The Valium was wearing off and she had forgotten to bring her aspen drops.

"*Is* there any gin?" she asked when Jeff finished.

Bob March arrived, apologizing for being late.

"Take a pew," said Jeff. "You're the first to arrive."

"Usually the first to arrive is the one who lives farthest away. Wanda's in the parking lot with the girls and Monty just pulled up."

At seven-thirty, the choir consisted of one alto, Wanda; one tenor, Bob; two (giggling) sopranos, Brianna and her chum Amanda; and two basses, Monty and the new recruit named Susan Moore, who would sing only on condition that she be allowed to sing bass.

("I can't tell you how many times I've been told a woman can't sing bass. I don't see why. I have the notes. At least the baritone notes," she told Chalice.

"Most directors won't even allow woman tenors," said Chalice. "It's a guy thing. You know, like boxing.")

"Well, there's a quorum," Jeff said. He propped open the piano lid and sat down on the bench.

Chalice directed everyone to pick up a choir folder and a piece of music from each of the five piles on the organ. Most of them had come from a full work day. Chalice surveyed them in the choir loft looking stunned from having managed to do one more thing. Most choir rehearsals started out a little subdued, but this group looked like a row of basset hounds. Chalice would have to leash them up and pull.

She was just about to start doing that very thing when Victor came out of his study at the far end of the sanctuary, carrying a sheaf of something. As he got closer, Chalice could see the blue choir music for "There Shall a Star Come out of Jacob." She looked at Jeff, her lips pressed together. An angry sweat seeped out all over her body.

"I hope that you won't mind trying it out, that's all," Victor said.

"Chalice is running this rehearsal." Jeff jumped up and took the music from Victor. "It's up to her."

Chalice turned her back on the two men and asked the choir to stand up and reach their arms up and out in a long stretch.

Victor touched her arm. "Why is Susan with Monty? She can't be singing bass!"

Chalice, incredulous, turned on him. "Victor. Get out!"

Jeff grabbed Victor's arm and walked him down the center aisle.

Chalice turned back to a choir that was now fully awake. The basset hounds had turned into terriers, sniffing with interest at the incipient drama. Her heart thumping, Chalice showed everyone how to do a yawn-sigh. She sat at the grand piano and ran a few scales for them, starting with C. It was on the E scale that she shrieked. Looking out at her, right around F-sharp-4, was the squirrel, its little eyes looking dazed, its little brain probably spinning.

Bob March was the first to get to the piano, followed by Jeff, who, having gotten Victor out of reach, sprinted up the aisle. Bob closed the lid of the piano carefully.

"Let's just keep him in there until we figure out how to get him out."

By now the whole choir had gathered around the piano.

"Should we get Victor?" Wanda asked.

"No!" said Jeff and Chalice together.

Chalice looked at her watch. It was eight o'clock. The rehearsal was to end at eight-thirty. It was her rehearsal and she was still sentient. Barely.

"Well, okay," she said. "Anyone here feel like touching a squirrel?"

There were some negative noises. Amanda and Brianna said, "Ewww."

"If I had some gloves and a sheet or towel, I'd do it," said Susan Moore's well-modulated baritone voice.

"I'll get the gloves and help," said Bob, and he was out the door.

He came back with two pairs of gloves, an old towel, and April, grinning.

"Congratulations, Chalice, you caught the squirrel. If Gwen were here, we might get a calendar page out of this." She sat next to Chalice, who had faded into the front pew.

Chalice leaned against her gratefully. "What a day this has been, what a rare mood I'm in," she said ruefully.

Everyone stepped back as Bob opened the piano lid. Susan threw the towel over the squirrel. She grabbed its small body through the towel and wrapped it up, holding it firmly.

"Get the door," she said.

Jeff charged into "For she's the jolly good fellow" on the piano, and Susan was sung out. After that, everyone was so utterly wide awake that the choir stayed until nine o'clock to warble and whine through five pieces of music.

"That was one memorable rehearsal, Chalice," Jeff said as he helped her straighten up the sanctuary.

She crosshatched the piles of music and folders and carried them into the vestry.

Jeff followed her with the cups of cold herb tea balanced on the stack of "There Shall a Star Come out of Jacob." He dumped the tea down the farmhouse sink and held up the stack of music.

"I'll take care of this," he said and winked.

Chapter Six

Maxine appears, Kimberly power walks, and April doesn't have to be so obvious

A week after Libby purged her photos, the boot finally came off her leg. She celebrated by pinning a favorite old glittery sunshine pin onto a well-worn denim jacket, pulling both legs into an old pair of jeans, and walking Callie five blocks down to the Preserve and Gather Café, renowned for their pickles and their welcome to well-behaved dogs. She texted Brianna to fetch Callie at the café when she got out of school.

She felt like an old familiar self whom she had apparently abandoned years ago. Callie, as though she sensed the enormity of the occasion, walked proudly beside her. She sat upright beside Libby's table, her head slowly moving back and forth as she surveyed the terrain on Libby's behalf.

Libby ordered the Pickle Plate. As she sucked at the pickled beet and looked at the worn places on her jeans, she thought about her student days, when she had probably bought most of the clothes she was wearing. When she was married, she dressed the part of the middle-class Christian, with well-tailored clothes and a squeaky clean look. Nordstrom Annex, people used to call the church she and Roger had attended.

Libby had buried her college clothes deep in the closet. At heart, she was a hippie. She had set out to be an artist. She had once had contacts in the publishing world and had done illustrations and cartoons. She wondered where her dry sense of humor had gotten to. Maybe she could recover it. She stroked Callie, who put her chin on Libby's healed leg.

"Such a beautiful dog."

Libby looked up at the speaker, a woman in a flowing paisley skirt, not unlike the ones Libby had been wearing for the nine months she'd been with the boot. A shawl in shades of green was pinned at the woman's shoulder with a large scarab pin. Above the pin, the woman looked to be in her seventies, with intense eyes and thick waves of gray hair.

"Yes, she is," Libby agreed. "Her name is Callie."

Callie preened at the sound of her name and thumped her tail.

"Do you mind if I sit here?" the woman asked. "I have a book to read. I won't bother you."

"Oh, please do bother me," Libby said, surprising herself. "I'd love a chat with someone who is reading Joan Chittister. I'm Libby."

The older woman arranged her skirt and shawl into the chair across the table from Libby. Callie sniffed at her.

"I'm Maxine. I've read Sister Joan for years. I met someone in here the other day who didn't know her writing but probably should. I rather hope I see her today. If she comes in, I want to loan this to her. She's a young woman who is trying to form a group in the neighborhood that would explore spirituality."

"Really?" said Libby. "That's unusual."

"It is. But I don't think she knows what she's doing, and I rather thought I might toddle over when her meetings start to see what she's gotten herself into."

"It's a subject that interests you?"

"My whole life."

"It has more or less chased me my whole life," said Libby. "But I don't know how interested I am. I just can't seem to get away from it."

"Maybe it hasn't found a way to express itself in you."

"How has it expressed itself in you?"

"I worked all over the world in the Peace Corps and in missions. I got used to seeing all kinds of spiritual phenomena, prescience, paranormal experiences — genuine and phony. I got used to sensing an unseen dimension. Now it floats in my mind alongside more common ways of perceiving the world."

Libby put her chin in her hand and stared past a rogue curl in Maxine's hair to the street outside the window. "An unseen dimension," she repeated. "What people mean by *spiritual.*"

"As opposed to religious infrastructure," Maxine said.

Callie sat up and thumped her tail. Libby turned her head to see Brianna come through the café door. Libby handed Brianna the leash.

"Shall I bring her back here?"

"No, I'll be at home."

Libby was in a meditative mood when she got home. She scanned her religious history for traces of what might be called spirituality. She had grown up in a conservative Christian home, where the emphasis had been on correct behavior and speech, neither of which included getting pregnant, having an abortion, and asking for emotional support. Maxine had used the word infrastructure. Religious infrastructure.

Libby sat at her desk and began to sketch. She sketched as much of Crown Hill Comm as she could see from her desk. Then she sketched a labyrinth from the point of view of someone lying on the ground and looking at the entrance. She sketched a cartoon-like labyrinth that meandered around April's yard, making an ostentatious detour around Rambles asleep in a patch of sun. She hauled out her old art materials and was busy playing with pencils and charcoal when Brianna and Callie came in. Brianna looked at the sketches.

"You should help April and Kay with their calendar."

Kimberly was power walking. She had both a reserve of energy to expel and a whir of thoughts to get under control. Some alarming part of her had risen up through the floorboards and was roaming her mind like an unwelcome relative: she was remembering the abortion she had undergone twenty-five years earlier.

When she was going through the envelope of photos, she had located Libby in a faded, crinkled group shot from years before. Kimberly had only a vague memory of Libby as someone who was going around with Victor. The clearer context was an afternoon at the women's clinic. They were alone in the purple reception area, waiting for their appointments and looking at editions of *Ms.* magazine and copies of *Our Bodies, Ourselves.* They were scared. They were there for the same reason. They had spoken briefly to each other.

Kimberly had repressed the entire afternoon almost immediately. But now it was running through her on a loop and she continued to recall details. The abortion had happened quickly. The room was warm and cozy. There was a collage of smiling women on the ceiling. The doctor and aides were women and had been gentle. Kimberly's body had handled the procedure with characteristic efficiency. She had gone into it stoically and come out relieved. By the time she went home to Phoenix that Christmas, the abortion was something that had happened to someone else, apparently the person who had just busted up through the floorboards of her mind.

Kimberly had only last week given a talk to her conservative Christian women's group — The Conservanteurs — about pro-life voices in Seattle. As she pounded along the sidewalk, Kimberly reflected that many conservative women had abortions in their past. Women didn't generally talk about them openly, especially not in conservative circles. Kimberly certainly never had. But after years of being a pastor's wife she wondered if every woman in the country had had an abortion at one time or another and just never talked about it.

Her more pressing qualm was what people — whom she imagined looked up to her — would say if this ever got out. She tried to imagine how that could happen. Well, first of all, Libby. Libby was an unknown. Libby had been at the church with April the day of that dreadful photo. April was not an unknown. Kimberly's face burned even hotter than it had already become what with the power walking. She could almost feel April putting it all together after one or two stray comments from Libby. By the time Kimberly reached Sandel Park and leaned against a tree to rest, April had already outed her, and everyone in town knew.

Her mind whirled. On the very rare occasions when Kimberly's mind whirled, she did the same thing: she pushed and shoved the material so that it became something else. Thus it suddenly occurred to her that Victor might have had Something To Do with Libby's pregnancy all those years ago. He had been evasive when she asked him about Libby. That in itself wasn't unusual, but there was an odd quality to his evasion that had put Kimberly's nose on a scent. It was a relief to sniff at it now and to stop thinking about all the people in the church who looked up to her.

She straightened up to resume her walk. Coming up on her right were two dog walkers. She recognized Corinne and Marvin, both dressed in army fatigues. Marvin, unleashed, bounded up to her, wagged, and then backed away. Kimberly pressed her lips into a sour smile. She hated that dog. Marvin jumped in circles around a border collie attached to a leash held by none other than Brianna Carpenter.

"Hello, you two." Kimberly put on her bright pastor's wife voice. "Brianna, I didn't know you had a dog."

"She's not mine." Brianna stepped out of the tangle Marvin had made of Callie's leash.

Kimberly collected her veneer and smoothed it around her. "Your mother told me you had a job. Is it a dog walking job?"

"Not exactly."

Kimberly and Brianna had always had a formal relationship. When Brianna was a child, she had had an unnerving way of staring at Kimberly. If she hadn't been a child, Kimberly would have called it disdain. Kimberly wasn't sure children were capable of disdain. Adolescents certainly were; her own daughter had been. She recognized the look Brianna was giving her now.

"It's a beautiful dog. Who does it belong to?"

"It's just someone I help with things she can't do because she broke her leg." Brianna looked down and rolled her lips into her mouth.

Kimberly's nose twitched. That scent again. But all she said was, "Corinne, such interesting back rests you made for the church pews. Unique."

"Yeah, why don't we kneel?" Corinne asked.

Kimberly did not want to get into a discussion about church practices with Corinne. "Maybe you will show us how," she said. It was the sort of thing Corinne might do anyway, without any prompting, in the middle of a service.

Kimberly began to walk again. A woman who broke her leg. Libby had a boot on her leg on the day of the photo. She had been with April, and April was an ill-advised mentor of Brianna. Kimberly walked home, got into her car, and put her baseball cap on.

Early evening, April looked up from dead-heading dahlias as Bob pulled up in his old blue Toyota Land Cruiser. Bob rode his bike to Nathan Hale High School every day of the year, regardless of weather. Today he had ridden home, changed into clothes already in the laundry basket, and driven off in Betty Blue. April clasped her hands to her heart and smiled in rapture as he backed the Toyota as close as he could to the front gate of their yard. She danced up to the driver's side as Bob opened the door.

"Who is the fairy god-person who gave these to you?" she asked.

Bob opened the back, where heaped on a tarp were enough paving stones for April to finish the last circuit of the labyrinth.

"The school secretary. They're remodeling." Bob looked pleased. He tugged on the tarp, which did not give way an inch. "We'll have to take them out one at a time until we can lift the tarp. Are you up for this?"

"You bet. I'll get my gloves." Inside, April strapped on an industrial strength bra and grabbed her heaviest gloves from her basket of gardening attire in the sunroom.

It took two hours to get the flagstones out of the Toyota and piled up at staggered points along the labyrinth route.

"This is going to be magnificent," Bob said as they deposited the last of the stones and looked at the meandering path. "So magnificent that maybe Victor will forgive you for poaching his idea."

"The consensus seems to be that he was never going to make a labyrinth anyway. But he still could. Nothing is stopping him except maybe himself."

"He's a big idea person. He needs a staff."

"Actually I think what he needs is a supervisor." April ruminated on this as she went inside for water. Victor had a supervisor: Kimberly. And a staff: Esme and the collection of church folk who thought he was wonderful. None of which did him much good. April shook herself. She didn't want to be thinking about Victor.

When she stepped back outside with two glasses and a bottle of Trader Joe's lime fizzy water, the nuisance himself was there, standing in the middle of her partially finished labyrinth, talking to her husband.

"Oh, hello, Victor," she said, deliberately not looking at Bob. "Want a drink?"

"Uh, no thanks, I just noticed Bob here, standing in what looks like an excavation."

"I was just telling Victor that you are creating a meandering path around the yard," Bob said, looking at her with a beseeching expression.

"A meandering path in pursuit of a labyrinth," April said witheringly.

"Really?" Victor looked around. "Not a classic labyrinth."

"Well, no. I've routed it around the fruit trees, the strawberry beds, and the little hillocks in the garden. And it makes an important loop around my forest of jack-in-the-pulpits." April couldn't help herself.

"So much distraction, though. It doesn't lend itself to contemplation," Victor said.

April narrowed her eyes. "Not sterile contemplation, no. How's *your* labyrinth coming?"

"I've had to postpone it. Things get busy this time of year, as you both know." Victor looked at his watch. "Which reminds me…" He held out his arms as though to bless them both. "Talk to you later, Bob."

"April, do you have to be so obvious?" Bob asked as they watched Victor cross the street to the church.

April looked at the fecundity around her, the extravagance of color and texture. All this beauty encouraged by her own hands. She looked at her husband, whom she sometimes felt she didn't deserve. She sighed her body into the tiredness of hard work and took a long drink of water. The solitary figure of Victor disappeared through the side door of the church. She felt a tiny flutter of conscience.

"No," she said. "I don't have to be so obvious."

Chapter Seven

The Ouroboros makes its first public appearance

Religion, spirituality, whatever you want to call it, the Ouroboros brings everything back to the beginning. So does a labyrinth. And a calendar. They end where they begin. It's about desire. Desire is the endless return.

Whether with desire, dissatisfaction, curiosity, or boredom, the first-nighters of Ouroboros were vaguely expecting something like church except with more comfortable chairs and better refreshments. Everyone who had ever been to church knew how to behave but few knew how to actually participate. April might have remarked that church people sit in pews like baby birds in the nest chirping, "Feed me, feed me."

The Ouroboros loomed large on the coffee table as Chalice fluttered around her living room, plumping pillows and lighting unscented beeswax candles. Its face seemed to have developed an impish expression. Chalice couldn't remember it having any kind of expression before this evening.

The first person to arrive was Maxine, whom Chalice had met at the Preserve and Gather Café where she had gone to get a wheat-free, corn-free, soy-free, sugar-free lunch. On that day they talked about the perils of being a Sensitive in a material world. Chalice had confided her nervousness about her upcoming Ouroboros experiment.

This evening Maxine had purposely arrived a bit early, judging correctly that Chalice would need a steadying presence. She was dressed in something that looked at first glance like a sari but turned out to be a graceful, flowing blouse of dark green with small explosions of bright yellow and blue. A yellow sunflower pin was anchored in her dark gray hair with a zigzag of a clip, also yellow.

The next to arrive was a woman named Sheila, who had visited Crown Hill Comm the single time Chalice had managed to get an announcement about Ouroboros into the church bulletin. Sheila was a transplant from one of the Carolinas and if you couldn't remember which one you were off her Christmas list forever. She was vocal in her hatred of the Pacific Northwest: people were unfriendly and phony. She walked, unsmiling, into Chalice's home and sat in a chair with her arms folded, determined to not find warmth and friendship in Seattle.

Wanda arrived, twisting her Coach bag.

Mrs. Fred Johansen II, known more commonly as Muffy, swanned into the front room, encouraged by the sight of Maxine, an older woman dressed — Mrs. Johansen looked more closely — not too oddly, sitting on the couch. Mrs. Johansen's husband was the deaf tenor in the church choir. Currently recovering from a hernia operation, Fred II was only nominally missed at rehearsal.

"Chalice," Mrs. Johansen adjusted her silk scarf, "I think it's marvelous that you are attempting to contribute to our church's spiritual life. I just hope this group is going to be Bible-based."

Friendlier faces arrived.

Kay: "My God, What's Bible Study Muffy doing here?"

April: "I'm only here to be supportive."

Bob: "I'm here because I'm interested."

"Thank you, Bob. That sentiment might be thin on the ground tonight."

"Oh, I don't think that's the case. You're attempting something out of the ordinary. People aren't sure what to think, that's all."

Chalice escaped to the kitchen for her aspen drops. She leaned against the refrigerator in the dark and tried to feel her breath down to her feet, which she told herself were on Mother Earth. She straightened herself and took a Singing Breath, which was considerably more spacious than a Spiritual Breath.

The last straw arrived: Kimberly. Chalice turned on the kitchen light and rummaged in a drawer. Kimberly appeared in the kitchen door as Chalice was dropping Rescue Remedy on the back of her tongue.

"Chalice, it's only me tonight. Victor wasn't able to come." She didn't mention that Victor thought she was spending the evening with her conservative Christian women's group. "He wanted to."

Chalice manufactured a smile. The words sounded menacing when Kimberly said them.

"Where is Chase?" Kimberly had wondered what on earth Chalice would do with her unruly son for the evening.

"He's with Kirk's mother. Kirk will be here soon but we're starting without him. This is really my thing."

The group assembled in the front room and stared at the Ouroboros. Chalice fussed with a rickety floor lamp and some unwieldy purple pillows before finally sitting down.

Maxine caught her eye and smiled. "Chalice, did you make your Ouroboros?"

"Yes, I did. At one of those do-it-yourself pottery shops."

"We used the Ouroboros symbol when I was in New Zealand," Maxine went on smoothly. "But we didn't have such a magnificent example of one."

Chalice couldn't have been more grateful for this opening, but heads did turn. Who was this rogue pagan with a flower in her hair who was treating this oddity as something perfectly normal when the rest of them had never seen anything like it?

"I don't think I know everyone here." Kimberly looked pointedly at Maxine.

"Yes, let's do some introductions," Chalice said. "I also want to get an idea of what people want in a group like this." Chalice picked up a clipboard and pen and waited.

As she looked at the Ouroboros, Mrs. Johansen repeated her preference that the group be Bible-based. Sheila said she was looking for a place to belong in this godforsaken area of the country. Everyone took this insult with the kind of sangfroid that Sheila despised in Pacific Northwesterners.

Kimberly was curious the way one might be on a reconnaissance mission, but she didn't put it that way. Her ears pricked as they were meant to when Kay said she was there because she thought the church needed an infusion of something. Wanda felt the same as Kay but hadn't realized it until then. Bob was there with the curiosity of a historian: why this, why now? April was there because Bob had dragged her there and she said as much.

"I want to know what this snake has to do with anything." Mrs. Johansen had started out uncomfortable with the sculpture but had positively squirmed when Maxine validated the creature. "In the Bible, you know what the snake was?"

"I think we all do, Mrs. Johansen," Chalice said. "But I want this group to be open to all traditions, and none of them will have any overriding authority."

Mrs. Johansen sat back and pressed her lips together. "I see."

"The snake is eating its own head," Wanda unnecessarily observed.

"Yes, it's the symbol of the Endless Return," Chalice recited.

"What does that mean?"

Chalice felt her hairline grow hot and her mind shut down. "It's a symbol I commune with." She could hear how pretentious that sounded. She had grown up in the Midwest. People from the Midwest didn't commune with symbols. Plus it hardly answered the question.

"Life is circular," Maxine offered. "We have seasons. We progress in spirals. Things come round over and over. We communed," she said, looking encouragingly at Chalice, "with those ideas when we worked with the Ouroboros in New Zealand."

"Like history repeating itself, only in microcosm, within ourselves," Bob offered.

Chalice looked grateful. Wanda looked bemused. Mrs. Johansen looked offended. Kimberly looked smug. Sheila, arms folded, looked at nothing. April played solitaire on her phone.

Chalice rallied herself. "I thought the Ouroboros would be the start of an altar. Next time we meet, people could bring items that have importance to them and we could all talk about them."

"I think that's an excellent idea," Bob said. "I don't know what your plan for tonight was, Chalice, but I would like to know how people define spirituality."

Chalice relaxed a little. This was more how she had hoped the evening would go. But there was a long silence. No one was used to defining spirituality, except Maxine, but Maxine felt she had said enough for the time being.

Mrs. Johansen finally declared, "The Bible describes the nature of God and of our proper relationship to Him."

As this remark was of a nature to kill all further conversation, there was a long silence.

"I'm sure there's more that can be said. The Bible represents one system of thought." Bob felt like he was in front of a classroom. It was exactly the sort of thing he said every day of his teaching career. "It seems to me that all the different religions are in their way trying to represent something that's common to them all, something that underlies them all."

"The more time I spend in the Bible, the more this underlying thing you mention comes alive." Kimberly was glad to say something edifying.

"That doesn't happen to me," Chalice responded. "The Bible seems dead to me, and nothing resuscitates it except a cross-reference from some other belief system."

"I hate that expression, 'belief system,'" Mrs. Johansen mimicked Chalice's tone. It was beneath her to do so but she really did hate the expression.

"Are you okay with 'something that underlies them?'" asked Maxine. "Because I think that's what's important."

"It's just that, if the word of God doesn't underlie everything, I don't see where you are. Where's your authority?" Mrs. Fred Johansen II had attended Bible Study Fellowship pretty much since its conception in the 1950s. She knew how to study the Bible and she was used to a format. This wasn't it.

Chalice sighed. She wanted to do her head launch but didn't think that would go over well. She put her hands together and drew them down the front of her body in a Virgin Mary pose. "We find our own authority within," she announced solemnly.

Mrs. Johansen sniffed. "That's not going to work."

"Maybe we could all take turns presenting our point of view and have discussions," suggested Kimberly.

April coughed.

"Well, whoever *wants* to present a point of view." Kimberly was already planning hers.

The doorbell rang. Chalice answered it. Voices murmured.

Heads turned as Libby came into the room. Bob looked sideways at April. April put down her solitaire game and looked at Kimberly. Kimberly's thoughts of her future presentation went into lockdown.

"Libby, how nice that you came," Maxine broke the silence.

"Come sit with us." April shoved Bob with her hip to make more room.

Bob sat on the arm of the couch so Libby could sit next to April. "Did April invite you?" It seemed unlikely.

"No, actually Maxine did. We met at the café."

Heads turned the other way. The exotic Maxine and now this mysterious stranger. Chalice felt the energy in the room teeter and spin. So did Maxine. Actually so did April but she would never have put it that way. She just knew that she was now glad she had come. She patted Libby on her arm and kept her eyes on Kimberly as introductions were made.

Kimberly put on her Minister's Wife Face: beaming interest and giving nothing away. Libby took a moment to decide whether or not she would meet Mrs. Kimberly May Kendrick Cummings on those tiresome grounds. Behind the benign face she assembled when Kimberly was introduced to her, she had an almost hysterical desire to ask, "Did you get that abortion?"

Instead she said coolly, "Yes, Kimberly and I have met. A long time ago. Hello, Kimberly." Her head moved gracefully. "Kay, nice to see you again. How did the photo turn out?"

April stifled a giggle. Bob poked her.

Kay looked doubtfully at them. "Fine. Nice to see you, too."

"I'm sorry to be late and interrupt everything."

The Ouroboros's expression had gone from impish to mocking. Chalice looked at Maxine and wondered what to do next.

The decision was mooted when the front door banged open and Chase zoomed into the house, his arms outstretched like airplane wings. In his flight through the room, he knocked over the rickety floor lamp. Kirk, right behind him, caught it before it landed on Mrs. Johansen.

Kirk and Chalice herded their offspring into the hall.

"What happened?" Chalice whispered.

"He wouldn't stay with Mom. I don't know why. I'll try to get him up to bed. How's this going?"

"OK, I guess. I don't know."

Chase's entrance brought the evening to a close. It was decided that Chalice would do the presentation at the next meeting and then Kimberly would take a turn. In the hubbub of coats and goodbyes, Wanda told Mrs. Johansen about the squirrel in the piano. A lavender folder which passed from Kay to April did not escape Kimberly's eye. As they bunched up at the front door, putting on coats, Sheila left with a perfunctory thank you to Chalice and walked slowly into the dark.

"What's her story?"

"Not sure. She came to church once or twice. She's determined to be unhappy."

"Libby, April and I can walk you home."

"Chalice, it was a little rocky but a good start. People need time to get used to creating something rather than having it handed to them."

"Do you want some help with the next meeting?"

"I'll bring cookies. Food always helps smooth things along."

"You'll come again?"

"Of course. I want to see Kimberly and Muffy explode."

Part II: OCTOBER

Chapter Eight

Kimberly gathers intel, Chalice has a scathingly brilliant idea and runs another rehearsal

"I saw Libby Cornish last night," Kimberly said.

"Who?"

"Oh, for God's sake, Victor, you know who I mean. Why are you pretending you didn't have a girlfriend twenty-five years ago?"

He was stretched out on the couch, watching football. It was Sunday afternoon. Kimberly knew he liked to decompress after morning services but she, in fact, was ready to explode. After leaving Chalice's meeting (she refused to call it Ouroboros), she came home to an empty house and went to bed early. The next morning Victor told her the squirrel had gotten back into the church and he had to meet Danny there at seven o'clock.

Kimberly had gotten through the morning service, staring at the second jagged aperture the squirrel had chewed in the wall. Like the first hole, which was still covered with swag, the second hole was also in the choir loft, this time where the sopranos stood. There was no choir yet, as there had only been the one rehearsal, but Jeff played something so magnificent on the organ that for once no one talked during the prelude. During the offertory, he accompanied Susan Moore's extraordinarily low voice singing, "Let There Be Peace on Earth," which brought Kimberly unwelcome recollections of the 1970s. She stared at the squirrel hole.

There had been no attempt made to cover it. As Victor duly delivered the sermon Kimberly had edited, he made an unauthorized digression to the squirrel hole in a complete non sequitur. Kimberly sighed. She was sitting next to Sheila, the Pacific Northwest hater, who snorted at the reference to the squirrel. Kimberly smiled in an attempt to be a friendly person, causing Sheila to move herself and her purse a little farther down the pew.

For the coffee hour, Corinne had brought something bread-like that she had baked: lumps of dough not unlike her kneeling pillows but without actually being festooned with bait-hooks. Kimberly put one on a napkin and walked around with it. She sipped at the weak church coffee and wore her Minister's Wife Face.

"Last night was quite an odd evening, didn't you think?" Mrs. Fred Johansen II bustled up to her.

"Well, it was the beginning of something Chalice wants to do," Kimberly said evenly. "It doesn't really have anything to do with the church."

"Except we were all there, weren't we?"

Wanda joined them, her Coach bag bumping Kimberly as she juggled her coffee and bread lump.

"What *are* those things?" asked Mrs. Johansen.

"They are actually better than they look." Wanda swallowed the bit she had been chewing. "What did you think of last night?"

Kimberly's mild smile started to feel to her like a plaster mold. "What did *you* think, Wanda?"

"I think I'm glad that Brianna didn't want to come with me. She doesn't need any more weird influences."

"Speaking of Brianna, I ran into her in the park. She was walking a dog and said she had a job."

"Oh, yes, the dog belongs to that woman who came last night, Libby. Brianna does odd jobs for her. Things she can't do because she broke her leg. Although she seemed to be walking around just fine last night."

"Are you talking about Libby?" Kay had appeared. "How do you all know her?"

Kimberly pressed her lips together to thaw them. Then she chewed the lower one. She needed to obtain information, not disseminate it.

"April introduced Brianna to her and now Brianna works for her. I don't know how Kimberly knows her," said Wanda.

"I knew her a long time ago," Kimberly said and immediately regretted it.

"In your former pastorate?"

"No, at school."

"That would be at Berkeley?" Kay persisted.

"Yes. You know, I need a word with Monty over there. Excuse me."

Kimberly didn't need a word with Monty. She needed to escape. She made a friendly-looking circle through the room, patting a few arms as she moved toward the door. She looked briefly around the fellowship hall, met Kay's curious eyes, pretended she hadn't, and slipped out.

She resisted the urge to get into her car, put on her Mariners cap, and drive north. She fished some walking shoes out of the trunk and went for a short power walk. Then she drove home, marched into her house, and interrupted her husband, lolling on the couch. "I saw Libby Cornish last night."

Victor sat up. "OK, she was a girlfriend. Briefly."

Kimberly was still standing. Her church clothes were disheveled. Her hair was plastered to her head with perspiration. Her hands were on her hips.

"Are you the father of her child?"

"What? No! Did she tell you that? She didn't have a child."

"Aha!"

"What, aha?"

"She did have an abortion."

"What?"

Kimberly paused. She had to be careful here. Libby had been in that Women's Clinic in Berkeley but so had Kimberly. It was this last bit that she wanted to keep to herself. She was so shaken by events of the last few weeks that she was afraid she might blurt out something. Something she didn't want out.

She grabbed the remote and pressed the off button. Victor looked helplessly at the television and then at her.

"OK, look. I was young. I was floundering around at Stiller Seminary. I met Libby while I was trying to decide if I was being called to the ministry. We dated for a while and then one night, we went too far. I was so ashamed and scared that I kind of disappeared."

"Was that when you decided you were called to the ministry?" Kimberly asked nastily. "After you lost your virginity and didn't say goodbye to the woman you impregnated?"

Victor looked horrified. "Who said she got pregnant?"

The horror cleared and Victor suddenly looked so miserable that Kimberly decided she had vented enough of her spleen to last her for a while. And she had managed to stay just clear of divulging anything of her own secrets. She relished her position.

"Can we go away for a few days?" she asked

"What do you mean?"

"Like to the mountains or the ocean."

"Would you like that?"

"Yes, I would. And as soon as possible."

Kimberly vouchsafed him the remote and left the room.

Sunday, the Martins had taken Chase and Kirk's mother to the mountains for the day. It had not been a success. By Monday Chalice felt like she had used up her mother units for the week. As soon as Kirk left with Chase to his all-day (thank god) kindergarten, Chalice called her Healer and had a long talk about her Mystifix-87 and her aspen drops. The Healer suggested Chalice try inversion therapy and walnut drops along with the aspen ones. She hung up from that conversation with a headache.

She lay down amongst all her purple pillows in the front room, with a moist lavender-scented cloth on her forehead. She meant to let her phone go to voice mail, but after it had rung half a dozen times she got up crossly and looked at the messages. Five from Esme. Oh, for God's sake. She put the phone in a kitchen drawer and went back to the front room couch. The doorbell rang. She ignored it. It rang again. She thought about answering it with the fireplace poker in her hand. A face through cupped hands pressed against the window by the front door.

"Chalice," a voice called. "I can see you in there. Is everything OK?"

Jeff. Chalice waved him in. Jeff in her front room was worth two days of Mystifix-87 in her body. He wasn't a child, a husband, a pastor, or Esme.

"Esme was going to march down here and make demands but I said I'd check up on you. And here you are on your fainting couch having the vapors," he grinned.

"I'm not comfortable with Esme knowing where I live." Chalice closed her eyes. "What the hell did she call me five times about?"

"Victor left unexpectedly for the week and she's been tasked with doing something more than playing FreeCell Solitaire. That includes finding a pastor for Sunday. She's trying to get a start on the bulletin and wants to know if the choir is singing."

"Why is Victor gone for the week?" Chalice sat up. Her head was already feeling better.

"I've no idea."

"We could do anything."

"We could."

"Or not do anything."

"True."

The phone rang.

"I suppose the first thing is to get Esme to stop calling. And I've just had the most scathingly brilliant idea." She went into the kitchen and came back with her phone to her ear. "Yes, the choir is singing. Put us anywhere you want, and the anthem is called 'Rain Down.' R-A-I-N. I don't care. The offertory slot is fine unless Jeff..." She covered the phone and looked questioningly at Jeff. He put one hand on his heart and swept the other toward her. "No, it's fine. You're welcome."

"*The Trouble with Angels*. Hayley Mills," Jeff said.

Chalice tossed her phone on a chair. "What?"

"'The most scathingly brilliant idea.' You got that from *The Trouble with Angels*."

Chalice blinked. "You're right, I did. What an odd thing for you to know."

"Why? I loved Hayley Mills when I was a kid."

"I don't really know you, Jeff."

"What do you want to know?"

"Anything. Tell me anything. Tell me your life story."

"Hmmm. I was born in Montpelier, Vermont. 1967. Started piano when I was seven and took lessons from the neighborhood piano teacher for eleven years. Mrs. Ringdall. I had a good ear. I taught myself guitar, banjo, harmonica, pennywhistle, saxophone, and tuba when I was growing up." Jeff ticked the instruments off on his fingers. "I studied music at the University in Burlington, wandered around India for a year and taught English in Nepal, learned to play the sitar, became a Buddhist. I came to Seattle to study jazz piano at Cornish."

"You're Buddhist?"

"That's right. Oh, and I'm gay. A gay Buddhist. I live with my partner, Chris. I met him in Nepal."

"Jeff, I didn't know any of this and I've worked with you for a year. It makes me feel like I've been high-maintenance."

"Well, you are high-maintenance, Chalice."

Chalice looked up. She thought she should feel offended but instead she found herself laughing. "I guess I am. I should just own it."

"Hey." He posed like a Buddha. "Be here now. Tell me about you."

"Oh, God. Well, I named myself Chalice. I had it changed legally after I graduated from music school. My real name is Manon. Can you believe that? My mother told people that she named me that because she adored Puccini. Except that the only opera she ever saw was the Massenet one — *Manon* -and technically all she saw were a few scenes being performed in a branch of the public library that she ducked into to get out of the rain while waiting for a bus. Manon. So affected." Chalice took a deep breath. "Not that Chalice isn't affected. More so, actually."

"I think you're a Chalice. I don't see you as a tragic opera character at all."

"Oh, that's so nice. I feel kind of mangled most of the time. You know, I've had relationships with both men and women. When I finally married Kirk, he really, really wanted a child. We went through a lot of sturm und drang about it. Course I go through sturm und drang about everything." It was such a relief to say so. "Why do you say I'm a Chalice?"

"Well, you're full, aren't you? There's a lot in you. You're intuitive, you sense a lot. The times I've heard you play the cello, it's melted me. You're good with amateurs because you have a respect for process and you're empathic. Those aren't often things one gets all in one person. It makes sense that you might feel all mangled until more of you gets sorted out and, oh, I don't know, Named."

Chalice looked down. Jeff's observations were a hair this side of too intimate. Much as she wanted to be noticed, it frightened her to think anyone actually did. There was a long silence.

"What's your scathingly brilliant idea?"

"You'll find out. I'm going to call Gwen and ask her to bring her camera. The ladies might like this for their calendar."

The scathingly brilliant idea involved some theatrics. The month of September had been warm and dry, but October introduced some rain, coordinating nicely with Chalice's choice of Sunday anthem, the aforementioned "Rain Down." Chalice couldn't stage manage the choir in the way she had planned if Victor had been around. He was such a fusspot about his services. The year before, she had tried to inaugurate a sort of scarf dance with palm branches on Palm Sunday and was immediately shut down. Victor could be as dramatic as he liked with his communion bread and clerical regalia, but no one dared crowd him on stage, except for Kay and her son with their astonishing altar tableaux. It would have taken an army of Puritans to stop them. Chalice wished she knew Kay better. It would have been good to have a force like Kay on her side.

There was a full choir attendance on the Thursday when Victor was out of town. Even the determined little squirrel put in an appearance. It darted across the back row of the choir loft as

Brianna and Amanda were coming in, causing them to squeal, and popped into its second hole above the soprano section.

"I'm not standing up there by that hole!" Amanda declared.

Chalice looked at Jeff. "Maybe we should reposition everyone. It's a little creepy to be up there with those two holes in the wall." She thought for a minute. "Actually, that gives me an idea."

"Another scathingly brilliant one?"

"No, just an elaboration on the first one."

"I hope I'm not the only alto on Sunday," Wanda said, bumping down the aisle.

"I'll sing with you. Wait, here's Gwen. Altos are here. Except I was really hoping Gwen would photograph us. Well, we'll make that happen somehow."

Susan and Monty arrived. Bass section accounted for.

Bob March came in holding two pairs of gloves and a towel. "Just in case we need to do another squirrel extraction. I heard our friend was back."

Jeff laughed. "I think it knows to stay out of the piano. It probably burst an eardrum in there."

Chalice assessed the space on the platform in front of the choir loft. She turned around and counted rows of pews and the choir members. Madelaine McGuffin came in while she was making calculations.

"Oh, good, here's another soprano." What she meant was, here's another adult soprano. Brianna and Amanda learned the melody part quickly and then just screwed around because Wanda, who was usually a repressive presence, struggled with the alto part right up to the second of performance.

Chalice smiled at the thought of the word *performance.* Victor objected to her characterization of "performance" as something the choir does on Sunday morning.

"What would you call it, then?" Chalice had asked him.

"It's a worship service. We are enabling worship. We don't perform," he had responded while fussing with his gaudy green and gold lamé stole.

"OK, places!" Chalice clapped her hands at the choir members, who were humming around Fred Johansen II. He had recovered enough from his hernia surgery to come in and sing deaf-tenor with Bob.

Jeff slid onto the organ bench and played the beginning of Bach's *Toccata and Fugue in D minor*. Everyone clapped or said "yeah, yeah" and looked at Chalice.

"I'm not sitting up there by that hole," Amanda repeated.

"No, you don't have to. We're sitting in pews."

"You mean when we sing?"

"I mean for right now."

"Where do you want the sopranos?"

"Are we going to be on both sides of the aisle?"

"Aren't we going to be too spread out? I like to be able to hear the tenors."

"Is there new music?"

"When do we sing in church?"

A shriek pierced the onslaught of questions. "There it is!" Amanda pointed at the squirrel hole, from whence a tiny, interested head poked.

"OK, listen!" Chalice grabbed at the silence. The squirrel was having a good influence in a weird sort of way. The choir had been subdued after its appearance last week. "Sit wherever you feel comfortable. Can we just get started?"

The squirrel stuck around through much of the rehearsal, sometimes watching from his hole and occasionally venturing out, only to pop back in when Amanda squealed, "There it is again!"

They sang the anthems that would get them through the rest of the year, Jeff at the piano and Chalice walking back and forth, listening and occasionally singing one of the parts. After half an hour of working the parts of "Rain Down," Chalice put the basses and tenors in the side aisle on the left and the sopranos and altos on the right. After singing "Rain Down" with this minor blocking, complaints rained down.

"It sounds different to me."

"I can't hear my part."

"The sopranos are flat and it's throwing me."

"We're not flat. You're flat."

"I don't want to do it this way."

"Nobody said we were going To Do It This Way. We're just playing around with an idea. Let's try it again from the front platform and, no, you don't have to go near the squirrel hole." Chalice squeezed Amanda's shoulders. "Stand in front."

Chalice waited patiently while everyone trooped up to the platform. Transitions with adults were not so different as those in Chase's kindergarten. Brianna dropped her music. She and Amanda started giggling and Wanda said, "Come on, girls." Fred said he didn't think he could do much more walking around so Jeff got him a chair. Gwen and Madelaine stopped in the center aisle to look at Madelaine's orange fingernails.

"Look how that shade is set off against the black and white of the music," Gwen said. "Very seasonal."

Wanda bustled over. "I found the loveliest girl to do my toes," she said.

Bob poked at a few keys on the piano. "Chalice, will you play the tenor line at measure twenty-five? I don't think I'm singing it right."

Chalice played the line. Bob sang it. Fred joined in a second time and Chalice played it louder. It was Fred who was all over the place at measure twenty-five.

"Thank you," she said in an undertone to Bob.

"Don't mention it," he breathed.

Chalice sang, "Hey, listen, everyone" with all the frontal resonance her mellow mezzo contained. "Let's try it again on the platform, and I want you to walk as you sing." Chalice held up both hands, stopping Amanda in an act of protest. "We're just going to experiment. Sing your part and move your feet. You don't have to go far, you just have to keep moving. One, two, three."

Chalice watched as her little bunch bumped around the platform. She and Jeff exchanged glances. This wasn't going to work.

"OK, here's the deal." Chalice passed around a clipboard. "I want everyone's current email. I want you all to bring an umbrella on Sunday morning and I want you here at nine o'clock sharp," she said. "I'll email a reminder on Saturday. Yes, I know, Fred, you don't do email. I'll call you."

"What are the umbrellas for? We aren't going to *sing* with them, are we?"

"We are just going to *try something different!* See you Sunday."

April and Kay visit the casino, Libby walks the labyrinth

"I can't believe we're doing this. I thought it was just a joke to bother Kimberly." April pulled her Ford Explorer into the Tulalip Resort Casino parking lot. The car smelled of manure and compost and was full of empty pots and detritus from April's first week back teaching at North Seattle Community College.

"It started out as a joke to bother Kimberly but then I thought, why not? It would make a good calendar photo," Kay said.

"Wait a minute," April braked in mid-maneuver into a parking space. "What if we run into Kimberly?"

"We won't. She and Victor are in Cannon Beach all week."

"How do you know that?"

"Esme told me when I went over for this." Kay pulled a church offering plate out of a capacious raffia bag. "I didn't expect to see her there on a Saturday but she's been putting in full days. She had to cancel things for Victor and line up somebody to preach on Sunday. She's done more this week than she's done in the entire four years she has pretended to work there."

April cut the ignition. "Sounds like Victor is no better at planning his vacations than he is his labyrinth."

"Oh, I don't think this was what you call planned. I think it's some sort of emergency intervention on Kimberly's part."

"How on earth would you know that?"

"Well, I don't really know anything. Something smells interesting. Did you know that your friend Libby knew Kimberly at Berkeley?"

April picked at a fingernail. "Yeah, I knew that." She felt Kay looking at her. She rummaged in her bag for a nail file.

"Did Libby know Victor, too?"

April smiled. Kay was an old hand at gossip. April rather enjoyed watching the expert at work.

"Was Libby an old flame?"

"You're too good at this." April started to open the car door.

"No, I'm just old and nothing surprises me. Hold it right there. We're not leaving the car til I get this sorted out." April closed the car door and looked at her nails. Kay was silent.

"Libby and Victor were together but Kimberly broke them up," Kay speculated. "No, that seems unlikely. Besides, I thought Kimberly and Victor met in Phoenix. But all of that seems pretty tame. There's something else, and something else usually means a baby or at least a pregnancy."

April looked at Kay, eyebrows raised. "It was the early 70s," she prompted. "Berkeley."

Kay furrowed her brow. "What? Protests?"

"You're getting cold."

"OK. Babies. Libby had Victor's baby. No, Libby got pregnant but didn't have Victor's baby. She had an abortion and Kimberly doesn't know about it."

"More or less." April felt less gleeful now that she was complicit in spilling Libby's secret. "Kay, you can't tell anyone."

"Who would I tell? And frankly, who would care? April, these things happen *all the time.* The interesting part is how people get their maxi-pads in a twist about it. The more religious you are, the worse the scandal. Kimberly must be…wait, there's something more, isn't there? How does Kimberly fit into this? She can't be upset just because some old girlfriend of Victor's moved into the neighborhood."

"You've figured out all that I know for sure. But Libby told me that she thinks Kimberly had an abortion at the same time she did. She doesn't know who the sperm donor was, but it wasn't Victor."

"Well, well, well, Kimberly the upright had an abortion."

"You *really* can't let this get around."

"Lips are sealed. It's a personal, private thing, I know, but it's nearly as common as menstruation."

"But all women menstruate. Not all women..." April stopped. "I guess a lot of us do get abortions." April went quiet. "I had one. After Nicholas."

"I've had two. One was even legal."

April looked out the car window at the people going in and out of the casino. "Life is a crapshoot. That could be the title of our photo." She looked at her watch. "Gwen is probably here somewhere."

"She's meeting us?"

"So she said."

They found Gwen at the slots, a small camera hanging around her neck. She was dressed in her usual black and white with one accessorized color, this time a necklace of large iridescent green Murano glass.

"What's the plan?"

"Well, ideally, I suppose we'd get a photo of one of us actually winning and money pouring into the offering plate."

"You don't actually get coins anymore when you win. Just little pieces of paper that you cash in." Gwen looked around. "Is it even legal to take photos here?"

"You know, I've never been in a casino," said April.

"Haven't you? Well, let's wander around a bit, take a little tour."

In the end Gwen got several photos of Kay and April pretending to win and a few surreptitious ones of various polyester activities in the casino. "I can Photoshop in whatever you want," she said.

"She's a wizard," Kay murmured to April.

"Yes, she is. Let's take her to lunch."

Since the day Libby had met Maxine at the Preserve and Gather Café she had been drawing. She did pencil drawings of everything she could see from her desk. She drew Callie. She drew Still Lifes that Brianna arranged for her. She drew Brianna. Then she drew them all over again in charcoal.

She designed a calendar for April and Kay. Brianna helped her reproduce her mock-up on the computer. She printed copies for April and Kay to see.

She hadn't felt this good in two years. Five years. Maybe ever.

Libby looked at the calendar pages. The one of Kay naked behind the hydrangea, the one of Chalice naked behind her hymn book with the fires of hell behind her, the one of Madelaine with her dress stuck in her underwear and toilet paper on her shoe, lighting the altar candle. They were funny because they were so shocking. But there was something more: there was a freedom that Libby envied. A freedom to laugh. An abandon to the humor of life. Yes, life is beautiful. Yes, life is sad. Yes, life is sacred. But life is also funny. And if a person believed in God — whatever that meant — she would have to believe that Funny was part of creation.

Libby's parents hadn't been fun-loving. They worked hard, went to a mainline church, and followed the rules of what was then the middle class. They would have been shocked at these pictures, without understanding why they might be funny. Five years ago Libby would have been both shocked and disapproving. Her husband leaving a twelve year-marriage to run off with some chippy without apparently planning to tell her, and then her running into Victor after all this time had frayed her sense of morality at its edges. She wanted that thing Maxine had talked about: the river she floated in or something like that.

She felt restless. She decided to see if April was home. She stuck her feet in some Birkenstocks, put on a colorful patchwork jacket, leashed up Callie, and set off down the street. In the traffic circle, Callie peed and sniffed. Libby looked warily at the church but there appeared to be nothing going on. She tugged at the leash.

April was not home. Bob was probably on his bike somewhere in east King County. Rambles was snoozing on the chaise longue by the sunroom door. He woke up, disapproved of Callie, turned over, and went back to sleep. Libby let Callie off the leash, told her to stay out of the garden beds, and pretended to believe she would.

The labyrinth was not quite finished but its entrance was marked with a footstool of a rock. Libby entered the outer circuit and began to walk. Deviations in the widest circle accommodated the fruit trees. The Cherry Bomb was empty of fruit but the plums and apple trees were loaded. She picked an apple, breathed on it, and polished it as she walked slowly through the turns. Leaves brushed against her face when she entered a loop that took her past April's magnificent old lilac trees.

In the deepest shade under the lilacs was a miniature forest of jack-in-the-pulpits now in their fall finery, their autumn surplices. A small bench was positioned so one could sit and look at them. Libby sat. Instead of a man in a pulpit looking down on a congregation, here was a congregation of pulpits for a woman to look down on. There were certainly more and more women pastors out there. What did a Doctor of Divinity degree do for a woman's ego?

Callie circled the bench and flopped down by her side. Libby absentmindedly stroked the top of her head.

Was it Christianity that was the problem? Libby had been taught that her life was a gift from God and there was a way He meant her to live it. In her religious education she had never been encouraged to feel her own alive-ness. She had been told how The Lord wanted her to think and feel and behave. That didn't create a river she wanted to float in.

She looked at all the little jacks in their pulpits. Sweet little guys.

Marriage. She didn't know many marriages that didn't diminish the woman. It was more than the impingement of living with another person. A woman was expected to give up hunks of herself that would have been considered unthinkable to a man. And then to swallow the chaser that this was her nature.

She breathed in the garden around her. April's passion for her plants was almost fierce. Libby wondered if the garden was an expression of April's determination to not lose hunks of herself in her marriage. Libby didn't see Bob as a pushover any more than he was particularly patriarchal. Well, no more than any man of that generation. But he apparently agreed that April had every right to be, well, a person. They seemed to have worked something out.

She heard a rustle in the grass and felt Rambles pressing against her leg. He purred and rubbed the side of his face against her. He jumped into her lap and looked inquiringly into her eyes. Libby smiled and touched her nose to his. Rambles curled up in her lap and continued to purr. Callie got up and cautiously sniffed at the cat, who tolerated being sniffed at by a dog. Callie pressed against Libby as she lowered herself to the ground. The three of them sat together for a long time.

Chapter Ten

It rains down, Victor and Kimberly come home

It was well and truly raining on Sunday when the choir assembled — late as Chalice knew they would be — with dripping umbrellas. She and Jeff had been there at nine o'clock and so had the visiting pastor, who turned out to be Pastor Muriel, a woman they knew and liked because her sermons tended to be short and to the point. Also she never stood in the pulpit. She stood in front of the pews on the same level as everyone else. Her main quirk was a husband who played the oboe and for whom she always insinuated a spot in the service at the last minute.

"Do you suppose Benton could just do a little bit at the end or the beginning or even the offertory? He has some music. I don't think the accompaniment is hard."

"Oh, I'm sure we can manage something," Chalice said. "Jeff, what do you think?" Victor would have been quite put-upon but Jeff was a jazz pianist and used to improvising. Prelude or postlude, it hardly mattered. Everyone talked through those anyway. But the offertory belonged to the choir.

"He could play with the hymns," Jeff suggested. Benton always needed a while to warm up and to suck self-importantly on his reeds. "And then do the postlude."

Chalice put the choir through a brief warm-up and then got them assembled with open umbrellas to rehearse "Rain Down." Fred Johansen II, still coddling his hernia sutures, sat in a chair. Bob held an umbrella over both of them and sang the tenor loudly into Fred's one good ear. Chalice backed down the center aisle to listen and watch. The choir's effervescent energy around the colorful props made them sing with spirit and more or less on pitch. "Fetching" was the word that came to mind.

"OK, one more time. Gwen, can you take a picture?"

The ten-thirty service was usually late getting started. Jeff always played the prelude on the organ because he could play so loud that people couldn't hear their own chatter. Then they came in, sat down, and shut up. He slid onto the organ bench and fiddled with the stops.

Amanda told Chalice she wasn't going to sing if she had to hold an umbrella. Chalice responded that if she didn't sing, Chalice would sic the squirrel on her. Amanda squealed and said, "Oh, all right." She sat in the soprano section, where Madelaine was painting Brianna's nails with her orange polish.

"Ooh, do me, do me," Amanda said.

"OK, but I have to finish Brianna before Wanda sees us."

April came, dripping in her gardening clothes, to the front of the church.

"I'm surprised to see you here," Chalice said.

"Bob texted me that it might be worth my while. He also said to bring these." She held out an umbrella, a yellow sou'wester, and an old accordion-pleated rain hat.

"Where did you find this? I haven't seen one of these since I was five!"

"It was in a drawer. That's all I know. Do I smell fingernail polish?"

"Probably."

"It doesn't smell like church, that's for sure. Maybe this will be worth my while."

Chalice scanned the sanctuary when the organ started. April joined Corinne and Marvin, it being generally accepted that Marvin was Corinne's therapy dog. Marvin had his teeth into one of Corinne's pillow lumps and was shaking it for all it was worth. Mrs. Johansen sat in the front pew so she could be Fred's music stand during the anthem. A small contingent of guests sat near the front in support of the visiting pastor. With them sat Benton, The Minister's Husband, nervously sucking his oboe reed.

In the choir loft, Wanda frowned at the nail painting. Bob tried to explain to Fred where he would sit for the anthem. He ended up shouting over the organ. The basses, Susan and Monty, sat quietly and patiently as basses always do, bless their hearts.

The organ became deafening. The congregation and choir settled down. The service had begun.

"Rain Down" went beautifully. Chalice wore the accordion-folded rain hat as she directed. No one dropped their music or put out anyone's eye with an umbrella spoke. Marvin got loose of Corinne and ran amongst the choir, barking at the singing umbrellas. Chalice picked him up and let him do the final cutoff with his front paw. Corinne cackled. The congregation clapped. This would never have happened had Kimberly and Victor been there.

The Minister's Husband couldn't sight-read the hymns. Chalice noticed that he sweat out the service until the postlude, at which time he shocked everyone with a loud and squeaky rendition of "Amazing Grace" that made Marvin howl. Amanda and Brianna giggled. Chalice set her face to listen politely but she was smiling into her hand when it was mercifully over.

While it rained down over western Washington in general and at Crown Hill Comm in particular, Kimberly and Victor drove home from the Oregon coast. It had not been a particularly successful getaway from Kimberly's point of view. The weather had been glorious. Their interactions had not been.

Kimberly forced Victor to talk about Libby. Had he known what had happened? Victor didn't have much to say. He just repeated that he had been young and scared.

"You know how it was back then in Christian circles," he said. "If you slept with someone, you thought you had to marry them. I freaked. What difference does any of this make? Why is it such a problem?"

"Well, don't you *think*? You're a pastor and Your Past lives down the street and she knows people in your congregation. Chatty people."

"They all aren't as judgmental as you are, Kimberly."

"What is *that* supposed to mean?"

"It means I am done talking about this."

Kimberly walked for hours, alone, on the beach. Victor had brought what he said was work but every time she came back from a walk, he closed his computer and turned on the television. He was depressed, she decided. *She* was depressed.

She ticked off all her worries when she walked.

The loan due at the end of January was the biggest concern, but thinking about money only made Kimberly sweat about her gambling propensity. That's all it was. A propensity. A way to relieve tension. It wasn't like a habit or a compulsion. When other things calmed down, she wouldn't feel the urge so often.

The squirrel was back in the church. It shouldn't be hard to get rid of a squirrel if Victor would only call some professionals instead of the Johansens' grandson. She was trying to stay out of it. Other people were on Victor about the squirrel. Muffy and Fred were all over their grandson. She could afford to let that problem run its course.

The calendar. First of all, she told herself, that calendar is not going to get made so I should stop letting it bother me. I just don't want those lavender folders falling into the hands of the church council. I wonder how many photos they have. Oh, gosh, Kay is on the council. I really need to talk to her about being discreet. She's not mean-spirited. I don't think she means to threaten Victor's position.

Victor's position. Every time Kimberly found herself having to worry about Victor's position, she felt resentful. It should have been *her* position. Maybe it wouldn't be such a bad thing if Victor's position was threatened.

They went out for dinner their last night at the ocean. Victor ordered an expensive bottle of wine.

"Since when are you so interested in wine?" she asked after listening to his fussy conversation with the sommelier about Chambertin.

Victor poured half a glass for her. "I'm not interested in wine at all."

It was the "at all" that put the wind up Kimberly. She couldn't very well mention she had been snooping around his office and had found the case of red wine. But she was on firm ground with her other discovery. "There's a case of white wine under the stage in the new wing. That's not communion wine. What's it doing there?"

"I don't know anything about it."

"Like you didn't know anything about Libby?"

Victor was silent.

Recklessness rolled over Kimberly like the waves on the beach. "It looks expensive. Who is buying expensive wine and storing it under our stage?"

The check came. Their debit card was refused for insufficient funds.

"How odd," Victor said. "I just put money into that account."

"I'll look into it." The reckless tide ebbed. She had pilfered that account for her last trip to Tulalip. "Here. Use my credit card."

That night Kimberly dreamt she was offered a poker chip as a communion wafer by a naked Libby. She shook herself awake and went to the kitchenette to make a mug of tea. Thinking she might go down to the beach, she was waylaid when she idly opened Victor's computer and saw a website devoted to Chambertin. She clicked through his history. He had also been looking at Malbec and Syrah. He wasn't looking for bargains. He was looking at vineyards and wineries and domaines and chateaux.

Kimberly might have balanced this information with her gambling, but so operative was her outrage that righteous amnesia took possession of her. Her Slight Gambling Propensity didn't even enter the equation with Victor's buying expensive wines ostensibly for communion when a final balloon payment was coming due on the loan.

They left the coast early in the afternoon and drove slowly, taking back roads and entering Washington through Astoria. A dreary trip in the rain, Kimberly didn't know why she thought it was a good idea other than it postponed having to actually solve the problems she had chewed on all week. It was dark when they pulled into their drive.

"We can unload and then I want to drop by the church," Victor said.

"Do you have to do that tonight?"

"You don't have to come. And you don't have to unpack. Just leave it and I'll do it."

"I'll go with you."

"Not necessary."

"Let's just go now." Kimberly was the one behind the wheel. She drove the mile and a half to the church and pulled into the alley outside the pastor's study. Leaving Victor rummaging around his desk, she walked into the sanctuary. She turned on the lights and walked slowly down the center aisle, looking in the pews. Hymnbooks and Bibles were all neatly racked. A pillow lump sat respectfully at the end of each pew. An umbrella leaned against the altar.

"Odd," she thought.

She picked it up and held it while she looked at the choir loft, the organ, the piano, the lady-of-the-harvest statue, which was the same plaster womanly figure that Kay and Jerry used for the Virgin Mary at Christmas. Now it was festooned like Carmen Miranda. Kimberly sighed.

She looked at the pulpit and wished it was her pulpit. She had so much to say. She mounted it and stood straight and tall, her hands resting in front of her.

"Father God," she started to pray. "I need your guidance."

She was just beginning to inform the God of the Universe of all that she was doing for Him when one of His other creatures, to be specific, the squirrel, flew out of the pulpit shelf.

"*Jesus Mary Fucking Joseph*!" Kimberly gasped and clamped both hands over her mouth. She backed away from the pulpit and looked into the shelf. There was a nest of paper shreds and droppings.

Kimberly burst into tears and staggered into the vestry, looking for tissues. Turning on the light, she saw three more umbrellas leaning against a chair and an accordion-pleated rain hat open on the table. Not finding what she wanted, she made her way into the church office, where Esme always had tissues next to a jar of some strange Amish clove-flavored hard candy that no one but Esme liked. Kimberly grabbed two tissues and stumbled through the side door onto Dibble Ave. She stood outside the church and sobbed.

What was happening to her? Kimberly never cried. She never gave up. She was never without a solution to the difficulties of life. She took a deep breath. "The Lord is my strength and my salvation," she repeated to herself. The part of her that didn't have a Slight Gambling Propensity believed this sincerely. The part of her that believed this sincerely didn't know she had a Slight Gambling Propensity.

Gradually she calmed herself and stood in the damp darkness. The rain had temporarily stopped and the world smelled fresh. Across the street a light was bobbing around in April's garden. The size of a silver dollar, it went up and down, disappeared and reappeared. What on earth?

Kimberly walked across the street. She heard rustling where the light was bobbing.

"Hello?" she said cautiously. She could make out a figure. "April?"

The light pointed into her face. "Oh, hi, Kimberly." April was in rain gear, a miner's light shining from her forehead.

"What are you doing?"

"I'm catching the critters that are eating my kale."

"Now?"

"They come out when it's damp and dark. There's one." She threw a snail into the street, where it landed with a crack.

The streetlight illuminated part of the meandering labyrinth. "Your garden is so lovely. I like all your paths."

"My paths." April went down on her knees and lifted a vine. "Oh, the labyrinth."

"The labyrinth," Kimberly repeated.

Victor strolled across the street. "What are you doing over here?"

"Talking to April. She has a labyrinth."

The question hung in the air: "Why don't *you* have a labyrinth?"

April stood with a squash vine and inspected the length of its stem.

"What are all those umbrellas doing in the vestry?" Victor changed the subject.

"How should I know? April, do you know what went on in the church while we were gone?"

"No idea." She was back on her hands and knees.

"Good news," Victor said as they walked back across the street. "We're advancing the retreat! We have our first rental group at the end of October."

"That might cover half a case of Chambertin," thought Kimberly.

Chapter Eleven

The Ouroboros smirks

F*or the second Ouroboros*, people knew to not expect church. Word had gone round that Kay was catering, so no one ate dessert before they came.

Chalice prepared her front room by chucking clutter into a closet and lighting the candles in the fireplace. She arranged the Ouroboros on the coffee table and it smirked at her.

"That's all you know," Chalice said to it, straightening its velvet cloth.

"Are you talking to me?" Kirk called from the kitchen. "Cause I can't hear you."

She went into the kitchen, where Kirk was watching their son dive-bomb peas into yoghurt.

"It's pee yoghurt!" Chase said. "Pee, pee, pee."

"You're letting him do that?" Chalice asked.

"Hey, I'm keeping food off the floor."

"Did he eat anything?"

"Pretty much everything except the peas and yoghurt as you see here."

"Chasie, will you stay with Grandma?"

"Pee, pee, pee," said Chase.

Chalice and Kirk looked at each other. "We'll see," said Kirk. "What are you planning for tonight?"

"We are going to do shamanic journeying."

"Is that that thing you learned to do that weekend last spring?"

Chalice sat at the table after Kirk and Chase left. She picked the peas out of the yoghurt, stirred in some Mystifix-87, and ate it. Then she cleared the table and loaded the dishwasher.

She changed into loose swami pants of a light apricot color and a black tank top that just skimmed the areolas of her breasts. She put little scarab studs in her ears and dangled her Venus pendant down her cleavage. She pulled on a diaphanous lavender shrug and hurried down the stairs to answer the door.

Kay stood with a stack of Tupperware. "I came early to help you set up." She took in her hostess's get-up. Kay was in her uniform of stretch jeans and one of a dozen colorful patchwork tunics she had made herself, pieced together with remnants from years of sewing. They covered her stomach and butt and were so eye-catching that people commented on them and Kay forgot to think about her stomach and butt.

"Oh, yes, cookies," Chalice said. She hadn't officially agreed to serve food to her spirituality group. It diluted the experience. "I guess you'll want tea."

"I can do that. I have a water heater in the car. I brought the tea. Do you think you have enough mugs? Cause April can probably bring some or I can get them from the church."

She bustled into the kitchen. Chalice followed and sorted through a cupboard of sippy cups, plastic glasses, and mugs. "I've got eight decent ones, I guess. If I wash the two in the dishwasher, that's ten."

"I'll do that." Kay opened the dishwasher. "How many are you expecting?"

"Um, well, last time there was you, me, Maxine, April and Bob, Wanda, Mrs. Johansen, that strange woman who's so unhappy — Sheila. Oh, and Kimberly. And Maxine's friend who came late. That's ten. I think I'll go commune with the Ouroboros if you're okay in here."

"Commune away." Kay waved her off. Strange girl, she thought. How does she exist in the real world? I'll call April and ask her to bring more mugs.

Maxine and Libby came in together. Then Wanda. April and Bob brought mugs. Mrs. Johansen and Kimberly arrived, their heads together, talking about something.

"Wow," said Chalice. "You all came back."

Sheila came in on the tail end of this sentence and felt slighted. She begrudged the entire city of Seattle the air that it breathed. She looked for a place to sit. All the comfortable chairs were taken. She sat on a floor pillow. It was just like the Pacific Northwest for people to not have enough chairs.

Wanda brought a statue of Our Lady of Guadalupe from her years in the mission field. "It was given to me by a woman whose baby I helped birth and it represents one of my good memories of being in Mexico." The thought of her good memories immediately made Wanda sad. She put the statue on the altar and sat down in confusion.

Mrs. Johansen brought a cross. "I want Jesus to be represented," she said. Privately she thought this was the greatest contribution she could make to this group. Jesus and maybe *Robert's Rules of Order.*

Kimberly brought a shell she had found at the ocean the week before. She didn't quite know what to make of Chalice's little spirituality group idea but she could never be far from the levers of control. She delivered an explanation for her shell that Maxine recognized as straight out of *Gift from the Sea.*

Bob poked April.

"No, you go ahead," she whispered. April already had her phone out.

"We brought flowers from the garden." He put a small vase next to the smirking face of the Ouroboros. "Amaryllis, so April tells me."

"Commonly called 'naked ladies.'" April didn't look up from her phone.

Maxine watched the altar grow and looked at people sitting self-consciously, sadly, uninterestedly, expectantly, and in one case defensively, with her arms folded across her chest. She was used to groups. She would never have told Chalice how few groups ever develop. In her heart of hearts, Maxine didn't give this one much future, but she had come to understand that wasn't the point. Nothing is ever lost. Relationships can form. Something can heal. Something can begin. New energy always percolates into the world.

The doorbell rang. Kay came out of the kitchen with a plate of cookies and passed Chalice on her way to the front door. "You didn't say when you wanted these, but everyone's looking like Corinne's pillow lumps in there. Food always helps."

Chalice's hostess's sensibilities were offended. How would Kay know what people looked like? She had been busy taking over Chalice's kitchen without being asked.

It was actually Corinne at the door, sans pillow lumps. She and Marvin were both dressed in camouflage. Marvin scampered in, did a turn around the room, sniffed at Libby, and jumped onto Bob's lap.

"Well, hello there," Bob said. "Just when I thought I would be the only boy."

That's blown it, thought Chalice. How would they do shamanic journeying with cookie crumbs and tea spills, Marvin running around, and Corinne popping her wad of gum?

Maxine stood up. "Are there drinks? Maybe you could use some help." She led Chalice into the kitchen. Sheila moved into Maxine's chair and crossed her arms across her skinny chest.

"Chalice, don't worry," said Maxine in the kitchen. "We'll get everyone fed and watered. They'll start feeling normal and then you can present whatever you have for tonight. What have you got planned?"

"I wanted to teach everyone to go on a shamanic journey."

Kay was back in the kitchen. "I'll take drink orders: liquorice peppermint or lemon ginger. Just two choices or we'll be here all night." She felt the sides of her battered old water heater, which whined and sneezed as the water inside heated.

Maxine sat Chalice down at the table. "Do you have a drummer?" she asked.

"You know about shamanic journeying?"

"Yes." Maxine smiled at a memory from years on a Cheyenne reservation in Montana. "Do you have a drummer?"

"I have a drum, but my arm's not really up to it for more than a minute or two. I was going to use a CD."

"How long did you imagine they were going to last?"

"I thought maybe half an hour for starters."

"Chalice, this is your evening, but half an hour of a drum beat is an eternity to people who have probably never even experienced an unguided three-minute meditation."

Chalice looked at the clock on the stove. Forty-five minutes gone in an evening that couldn't go past two hours. She was never at this kind of loss when she was doing music. Why did she think her skills would cross over so?

"Can I make a suggestion?"

"Please."

"Why don't you have them work up to three minutes of silent meditation? Start with a minute, then two minutes, then three."

"Really? That doesn't seem all that much."

Maxine leaned back and looked into the front room. Bob was making Marvin jump for a cookie and Corinne was cackling. Kay almost tripped and dropped a tray of mugs but Libby caught her just in time. April, on her phone, was oblivious to it all.

"I think three minutes should just about do it," she said. "Do you know how to explain a silent meditation?"

"Not really."

"I learned silent meditation when the only instruction was to listen to your breath. We tried it cold and then talked about what kind of experience we had. It certainly was instructive for me at the time."

"Like a first rehearsal with a new choir or orchestra," said Chalice. "You find out what's there. I think I can do that."

April used an app on her phone to time the meditation. After the first minute, everyone except Maxine and Libby claimed that they had been able to focus on their breathing for the full minute.

"I'm out of practice," Maxine said.

"I never was able to do this," Libby said.

After these revelations, everyone else admitted that maybe they hadn't quite stayed with it for the full minute.

"Who knew a minute could feel so long?" asked Mrs. Johansen. She found this interesting in spite of herself.

Libby said she used to count to ten on the inhale and count to ten again on the exhale. They all agreed to try this for two minutes even though Libby repeated she had never been successful.

"Count *silently*," Kimberly hissed to Corinne once they had begun.

"Sorry," whispered Corinne. She chomped her gum while she counted to herself.

"*Stop chewing*."

Marvin yawned and all his collar tags clinked.

It took Kimberly a full minute to stop feeling annoyed at Corinne.

After the two-minute meditation, Chalice said she had imagined an up bow for the inhale and a down bow for the exhale. She was quite pleased about this. Wanda said she felt more relaxed and asked if that was the point. Sheila silently wished she were back in South Carolina where no one would dream of spending an evening not talking.

"I've been closing my eyes. Can we look at something?" asked Bob.

The suggestion had been made, so no one could resist trying the three-minute meditation with their eyes open. Kimberly looked at her shell and made mental bullet points of her own presentation to this group next month. Wanda looked at Our Lady of Guadalupe and her eyes filled. She closed them. Tears rolled down her cheeks. Mrs. Johansen looked at the cross and thought about Danny and the squirrel in the church. It was a slur on her family that he hadn't gotten rid of it. Now that Fred was home from the hospital and starting to do things, maybe he could help trap the thing. Kay dozed off. Bob stared at the Ouroboros and watched his thoughts come and go like a historical procession of events. He rather enjoyed the sensation. April quietly went back to her game of solitaire. Libby gave up the attempt altogether, looked with curiosity at Kimberly, and wondered about that long ago day in the clinic.

When April's phone dinged, everyone shifted in their chairs. At the evening's close, they congratulated each other that they had done quite well with focusing on something.

The squirrel family takes up residence,

Kimberly melts down, and April has to put up with it all

Spring and fall were the busiest times of April's year. Along with a full teaching load, in the spring she had the garden to plant and in the fall she had the garden to put to bed for the winter. She was engaged with the latter the day before Halloween, the same weekend in late October that Crown Hill Comm was hosting its first rental group in the new wing. Ordinarily, April (and the dog-walkers) could enjoy the garden until well into November but the warm fall suddenly took a blast from the north and the autumn started to pass away. A cold front came through and put the dahlias into mourning.

April was taking down the blackened dahlias inside the front fence when cars began pulling up to the church late Friday afternoon. Bags and suitcases were disgorged from trunks and back seats. Boxes moved from the car to the church steps. April, ratchet pruning a particularly tough stalk, didn't see the approach of a woman in purple leggings and a pink ski coat.

"Excuse me. I wondered if you knew anything about the church across the street," said the purple leggings. "We expected someone to be here to let us in but all the doors are locked."

April cursed to herself. God, they were a bunch, that church. Who were these people, anyway? How fast could she get them out of her hair? She could say she didn't know anything about the church and, oh, how she wished she didn't. She could call Kay. Kay liked to feel needed. She could call Bob. It was his church, after all. He could be the resource for however long they were there and whatever they wanted. He had a key to the church. April even knew where it was but this was not her problem.

In the end, she called them both and let the God-botherers sit on the front steps of the church and wait. The sun was out. They'd live.

Kimberly and Victor came screeching up to the church before either Bob or Kay got there, Kimberly in her Legacy and Victor in his secondhand Cadillac with the vanity plate "DOCDIV." They hustled around the corner to the front of the church, where April could hear the profuse apologies but couldn't see the abasements and flagellations. She went back to her work, nearly stepping on Rambles, curled up amongst the stocks; he flattened out a private cave no matter how much April tried to discourage it. He leaped out of the garden and onto the flat stone that marked the entrance to the labyrinth. He licked his paws.

The sun dropped in the west, no longer sending its long shadows through April's lilacs and across the yard. Rambles followed her into the house. He leaped into the sink. April turned on the faucet. Bob always let him have a good stream of water but April set it back until it was barely a trickle. She was a gardener and observed water conservation at every level. Rambles looked at her disapprovingly but she ignored him. He sat without drinking, staring pointedly at the miserly stream. Finally he jumped out of the sink and drank from a water bowl in the pantry, one of the five staggered around the house for his private use. April turned off the tap.

Kay arrived. A lavender folder stuck out of her raffia bag.

"They got into the church all right, then?"

"Yeah, Victor and Kimberly finally arrived. Do I even want to know what's going on?"

"It's the first rental group in the new wing. They are having a Christian un-Halloween tomorrow."

"Really? How not interesting."

"Look, I want you to see these photos." Kay pulled the lavender folder out of her bag.

They sat together at the table.

Kay was so sweet, April thought. She dealt in hard copies because she didn't know how to email photos.

The first photo had been beautifully Photoshopped by Gwen. It showed April and Kay in a tug-of-war with an offering plate filling with money that poured out of a slot machine. In the background was a woman in a polyester pantsuit with a cigarette hanging out of her mouth and three men with bellies grouped around a roulette table.

April laughed. "What's the caption?"

"I don't know. Showers of Blessings? God Shall Supply All Your Needs?"

"Or what you said at the casino: Life is a Crapshoot."

"All good. Except that's a slot machine." Kay continued, "Now look at these. What do you think?" There were five or six shots of the choir with their umbrellas: Fred Johansen in a chair and Bob holding the umbrella over him, Chalice in her accordion-pleated rain hat, Marvin running around, Muffy Johansen looking on in disapproval.

"Oh, these are fun," April said. "When did Gwen do this?"

"She slipped out of place while they were singing in the service and took them."

"Really? I didn't notice."

"You were probably playing solitaire on your phone."

"I wasn't! So, got any gossip?"

"Victor got one of those plastic labyrinths. He's laid it out in the round room."

"Well, well, he got his labyrinth after all."

Through the window April saw Bob wheeling his bike into the sunroom. He took off his gloves, shoes, and helmet and poked his head into the kitchen. "I'm going over to the church to give them a hand. It seems that squirrel actually has a family and they've set up housekeeping in one of the rooms of the new wing. I've never seen Kimberly so angry. I thought she was going to yank Victor's arm right out of its socket. Can I send her over here to calm down?"

"No!" both Kay and April said.

"Oh, c'mon, April."

"Oh, all right. But make it a casual suggestion. And if she starts to take out Victor's tongue, let her finish."

Kay put the photos in the lavender folder and stuffed them into her bag.

April guessed that the suggestion had not been at all casual when Kimberly came in the kitchen. She had the look of someone who had been forcefully marched across the street. Her face was red as a pepper (a Red Savina, April thought) and her hair was sticking out like Phyllis Diller's. Mascara ran down one red cheek and smudged the eyelid of the other. Her sage-green blouse was unbuttoned in three places, coming out of her skirt and revealing an immaculate white slip and bra.

April rotated her toward the bathroom off the pantry and gave her a clean washcloth and hand towel.

Back in the kitchen, Kay mouthed the word, "Wow!"

"I know," whispered April. "Who wears a slip anymore?"

They waited in reverential silence until Kimberly came out of the bathroom. Her face was clean and her blouse was buttoned but she didn't seem any calmer. She was evidently still in full flight.

"What happened?" prompted Kay.

Kimberly sat at the table and rubbed her face with her hands. “The one thing, the One Thing I didn’t remind him of over and over and over and over — ”

“You mean ‘nag?’”

“ — was the squirrel. He wouldn’t call a proper pest control. He had to ask Fred and Muffy’s useless grandson. And now we’ve got two holes in the sanctuary, a nest in the pulpit, and squirrels in the wing. It’s going to have to be cleaned, repainted, and re-carpeted. AND he’s got that group over there who are now going to stay the weekend for free. I told him he was in sole charge. I’m not on call. Oh, dear God. Somebody was screaming at him in front of the group from Luther Memorial and I think it was me.”

“You know, pest control doesn’t handle squirrels,” offered Kay. “You need to call a trapper.”

This bit of information appeared to calm Kimberly. April could understand that. It was a piece of practicality to grab hold of. It was something concrete to do.

“Thank you. I’ll remember that.”

“Why don’t you take some time off?” April looked around her kitchen and out the window at her front garden. “Go away.”

“We just came back from a week at Cannon Beach.”

“I don’t mean the two of you. I mean just you.”

Kimberly put her chin in her hands and gazed at nothing. She chewed her lip. She turned her head, her eyes following something.

April turned to look out the nook window just in time to see Libby and a dog’s tail pass the side of the house. The sliding door to the sunroom opened and Libby was heard to say, “C’mon, Callie.”

Kimberly pressed her hands against the table and stood up. “I’ll give it some thought.”

“Knock, knock,” said Libby. She had a file folder in her hand. Lavender. “Am I interrupting something? Oh, I see I am.

April, I'm bringing you an um..." She looked inquiringly at April and Kay.

Kimberly sat back down. "Yes, let's talk about the calendar," she said.

"She actually handled it better than I thought she would," April told Bob that night. "She stayed calm. She looked at the calendar pages. The photos look more respectable when they have a context. They have more gravitas."

Bob looked at the photo of his wife and Kay fighting over an offering plate at the casino.

"Yeah," he snorted. "That's what they have now. Gravitas."

April sat on the edge of the bed with him. "That one gave her a start. Her face went all red again, I guess when she recognized the casino. Then..." April started to laugh. "Then all she said..." April fell backward onto the bed, laughing. "All she said was, 'Is that a church offering plate?' I thought Kay and I were going to explode."

"What do you mean, she recognized the casino?"

"You don't know?"

"I guess not."

"Kimberly has a gambling habit."

"April, where do you pick up this stuff?"

"Well, let's see. I think I first heard it from Kay, and then Corinne said she had gone once with Kimberly."

"Corinne. OK, let's say Corinne actually went with her once. Does that mean she has a habit?"

"I don't know how Kay knows things, but she's usually reliable."

"It's a struggling little church," Bob said.

"Yes, I can see why." April went into the bathroom. "Would you mind if we used that photo of the choir with the umbrellas? The one you're in?"

"Can I stop you?"

"No, but Gwen can change your face."

"You can use my face. I can't speak for anyone else. What was Kimberly's verdict on the calendar?"

"Well, there's nothing she can do about it if we don't actually advertise it as Crown Hill Community, the struggling little church that needs to put out a cheesecake calendar in order to pay its bills. I wouldn't expect a gambler to pass up a chance to make some money. The odds are at least as good as the slots at Tulalip."

A phone dinged.

"Nicholas just texted. He's definitely coming for Thanksgiving."

"Oh, good!"

Chapter Thirteen

Kimberly makes a retreat, and Chalice has an audition

On the Saturday morning of Halloween, Kimberly was hard at work in the home of a friend from The Conservanteurs, her conservative women's group, where she had spent the night after her explosion at the church and subsequent cooldown at April's house. She had awakened early and made a pot of coffee. Now she sat at her computer, with ideas flying out of her faster than she could type.

It was her turn to lead Ouroboros. She planned to come in with something considerably more useful (and necessary) than meditating over a snake. She had been awake a good part of the night thinking about the calendar photos she had seen in April's kitchen. Images had attacked her dreams, especially the one in the casino. Kimberly relived the alarm she had felt when she saw the slot machine photo. Her mind had fixated on the fact that someone (Kay) had taken an offering plate out of the church.

This calendar went beyond irreverent. It went beyond sacrilegious. It was tasteless, no, it was obscene. Conflating the calendar with yet another rogue church offshoot, That Snake Group, she decided what everyone needed was a good dose of

Bible. To this end, she thumbed her worn and notated Bible and scoured the internet for verses. She copied and pasted chunks from different translations and versions into a document: Operation Godly Behavior.doc.

Ah, here was a good one. *The Message* version said it best: "Don't be flip with the sacred. Banter and silliness give no honor to God. Don't reduce holy mysteries to slogans." Matthew 7:6.

Another good one: "You were bought at a price. Don't be enslaved by the world." First Corinthians 7:23.

Here's one for Kay: "Older women likewise are to be reverent in their behavior, not malicious gossips." Titus 2:3.

More from Matthew 7: "Don't pick on people, jump on their failures, criticize their faults — unless, of course, you want the same treatment. That critical spirit has a way of boomeranging. It's easy to see a smudge on your neighbor's face and be oblivious to the ugly sneer on your own."

We don't need to get into that, she thought. That's a slightly different theme. I think I'll call my talk "Moral Excellence." But I like "Operation Godly Behavior." Slightly old-fashioned idea, I guess, but I think that's what's called for here. Now I need an activity.

She decided to have a big pad on an easel and take marking pens so they could cull their (her) ideas as a group. She thought about passing out index cards to gather up individual ideas but nixed that idea. She wanted to *guide* the evening. Yes, that was the thing to do. Not control, but guide. Index cards were too freeing to the spirit. Once they had gotten all Kimberly's points up on the pad, they would create something to enshrine them on. Like a bookmark.

Or they could all start a journal. Now there was an idea that might give her a wedge into influencing Chalice's group on into the future, maybe even take over when it inevitably petered out. Chalice clearly had no idea of how to run a meeting.

Or — and here Kimberly had to hold onto her chair because she thought she was being raptured and she didn't want to leave earth until she had enacted her plan — they could all create A Calendar! Twelve months of moral excellence, godly comportment, and Biblical behavior. A calendar! Wouldn't that just frost them all?

By noon she had sketched out the entire evening, including how everyone would behave and how vindicated she would feel. Then she sat back and drank the last of her coffee, which had been stone cold two hours ago. OK, this might be a little overwrought, she thought. But I think I have the core of it.

She got into her car, put on her Mariners cap, and drove north.

Chalice also drove north on the Saturday of Halloween. While not precisely running away from home, she was advancing a rather daring idea, the seed of which she had gotten from April the afternoon Chase had wheeled all those rocks for the labyrinth. April had managed him like he was one of her plants while Chalice sat there holding a sticky juice box instead of a box of rosin.

"If something in the garden isn't flourishing, you either pull it up or move it," April had said. She had also said that there was nothing wrong with Kirk being The Mom. One other remark had stayed with Chalice: what April had said about Victor. "I've never seen anyone less suited to his job."

Chalice couldn't agree more. He was such a pain. He had asked her *again* about that stupid Mendelssohn. How many times had that come up? Between her and Jeff, he had probably been told no a dozen times. What does he hear? she wondered. Now he was all over her about the Christmas music. He had asked her to work with him on the children's pageant. He thought the children could use some coaching on the parts they sang but Chalice had demurred. Jeff could manage a few bon mots for them since he was accompanying them on the piano.

"I thought you might want to be part of it since you're a mother," Victor had said. "Since Chase is in the pageant."

Chalice had looked at him witheringly. "Since Chase is in the pageant, I would like to be able to watch it."

Neither of us is suited to our jobs, Chalice thought as she drove north. And I am not flourishing.

Chalice was driving to an audition. She had called the University of Washington music department and had gotten names of cello teachers in the area. Now she was on her way to audition for a place in the maestro's studio. She wanted to work with a good teacher for a while and get her skills and confidence at least to the level they were before she had Chase. Then she'd start auditioning. She wanted gigs. More than gigs, she wanted a chair in an orchestra. She was a plant that needed to be moved.

Chase and Kirk are fine, she reassured herself. They've got Halloween ahead of them. I don't have to worry. I'm lucky to have Kirk since I'm so high-maintenance. She smiled, remembering Jeff's candor. I'm lucky to have Jeff, too.

The new wing opens for business and Libby takes a walk

April approved of any holiday that utilized a plant. Oxalis for St. Patrick's Day, lilies-of-the-valley and sweet woodruff for May Day, lilies for Easter, gourds for Thanksgiving, holly and ivy for Christmas.

Pumpkins for Halloween. Usually she planted them along the edge of the garden and trained the vines to grow away from the bed, so that by Halloween pumpkins polka-dotted the yard. This year she had rerouted them so she could lay the labyrinth, and a great many of them were now growing outside the fence. Two bloated white ghost pumpkins somehow got themselves stationed in satisfying symmetry on either end of the front gate. Small sugar-pie pumpkins gamboled with jack-o'-lantern-sized ones in a cheerful jumble of orange, yellow, ghost-white, and deep green. A granddaddy of orange pumpkins — the biggest April had ever grown — positioned himself like a sentinel near the front gate. Hollowed out, a child could fit inside of it.

On the morning of Halloween, April photographed the front of her house. Rambles had jumped onto the giant pumpkin and posed. Then he picked his way delicately through the smaller pumpkins. Standing in the street, April stopped traffic, her eye to her camera until she caught his lovely orange and white fur shining against the dark green of the vines.

She pocketed her camera and returned to the front gate, where she dropped to her hands and knees to sniff the three largest pumpkins for dog pee, the first whiff of which would bring out one of her signs. She had a whole collection, ranging from polite to sarcastic. She didn't smell any pee, but for the holiday she put out a sign anyway: "Biscuits for all dogs who don't pee on edibles." For the most part, April had the locals trained. It was the dogs that came from neighboring areas — as they did on holidays and weekend mornings — that needed minding.

Her nose was near the ground when two purple ankles came into view. She sat up to a Styrofoam cup of coffee and a Krispy Kreme doughnut. She looked up to a face beaming out of a pink puffy coat.

"Good morning. I wanted to thank you for your help last night."

"It was nothing."

"We're the Northshore Luther Memorial youth group and we're having an un-Halloween party at the church tonight."

There was a pause. Does she expect me to ask what that is? April wondered.

"I bet you're wondering what that is."

"Not really. I think I can figure it out. Thank you for the coffee."

"We've been talking about the concept of a labyrinth, and I couldn't help but notice you had this outdoor one over here. You were so kind last night and since you're members of the church, I thought I'd just ask if you might let our group come across the street and walk it?"

April was horrified. She readied herself to draw a mark and tell this pink creature to not put a purple toe over it. Everyone at North Seattle Community College, from her students to the office assistants to the dean himself, was familiar with the look now on April's face. Even Victor, who was nipping across the street and who was oblivious to all nuances of human expression, looked alarmed.

"Perpetua! You're wanted inside. Morning, April. Is Bob at home? I was hoping to talk with him."

"He's on a ride. A long one."

Victor continued to stand where April was fussing with her pumpkins outside the fence. He was hard to ignore because his shoes were in her line of vision now that the purple ankles were gone. She stood up and started toward the house.

Victor suddenly said, "Kimberly didn't come home last night."

April froze, staring at her gate, so near and yet so far. She sighed and turned around. She looked at Victor and saw, to her surprise, the crestfallen face of a fourteen-year-old boy. How many times she had seen that face on her son. Inside her, something maternal felt out of place, rather like a volunteer potato in the brassicas.

"She was pretty angry last night. She probably just needed some time to cool down." She moved closer to her gate.

"This weekend retreat thing is a mess." He looked over the fence at April's garden. "Your labyrinth is beautiful."

Thinking he was about to ask if his un-Halloween retreaters could walk it, April said, "The meandering paths, thank you." How was she going to end this? She tried to imagine what she would say if the face before her had been Nicholas. "When a plant isn't flourishing, I move it." She wouldn't have put it like that to Nicholas. She would have simply moved heaven and earth to help him find a place he would flourish.

"What do you mean?"

"You're not flourishing," April said bluntly.

On Halloween night, Libby took Callie for a long walk through the neighborhood. She liked to see the jack-o'-lanterns glowing on front porches. It was the only tradition left from the old days when Halloween was purely a kid's holiday and the only adult participation was carving the jack-o'-lantern and manning the candy bowl at the front door. As they circled through the neighborhood they encountered small groups of costumed children escorted by large groups of adults with cameras. Their masks askew, the children had to be led, or they wandered off sideways. Libby and Callie came to rest on the first bench inside Crown Hill Cemetery, where they could still witness the procession.

On Halloween back in the day, you could run wild through the neighborhoods, two by two, going methodically down one side of a street and up the other, filling your bag to bursting, leaving it off at home and heading out again with an empty. Everyone gave candy. You never got fruit except sometimes small boxes of raisins, which the kids despised. Libby's favorite had been Tootsie Roll Pops. The year she was nine — the year her costume was, depending on who you asked, Queen Esther (her mother) or a harlot (Libby had just learned the word) — she collected fifteen full-size pops and in the flavors she preferred, that is to say, the bright-colored flavors, not the brown pseudo-chocolate.

She stretched out her leg and massaged it before getting up again. She and Callie did a loop through the cemetery until they came to a hidden gate in the fence that opened onto the March property. Libby's fingers found the latch, and she let herself and Callie into April and Bob's yard. The house was dark and the gate was shut. A large bowl of bite-size Snickers and 3 Musketeers bars was nearly empty outside the front gate.

She clicked the gate shut behind her. April probably had not wanted to be near the un-Halloween party.

They walked past the new wing of the church. There were the two rooms, one dark with shades drawn — that would be the squirrel's residence — the other lit. The large hall was fully lighted. A meal was being prepared. Women were officiating. Victor was spinning around in a chef's apron, apparently trying to assist and combing his hand through his hair that was no longer there. Libby walked on, glad to not be part of it.

It had been interesting, sitting at April's kitchen table last night with Kimberly right there. Libby realized that she didn't actually have anything against her. Her only memory was of sitting in the waiting room of the Women's Clinic with her for half an hour. The rest was just comments in the wind: Kimberly Kendrick was not a "women's libber;" she was a traditional type. Legalistic was a word they sometimes used back then. She spoke out against abortion, which had recently become legal. Then she apparently had one and went home to Phoenix.

No, it was Victor she had all the energy around. Victor whose presence now, even if only tangential, had broken open an old wound. She already knew she had conflated Victor with her ex-husband and she didn't care. They could both go to hell. But there was no reason to include Kimberly.

At first her only question about Kimberly was whether her (alleged) abortion had softened or altered her in any way. Now it occurred to her that Kimberly might feel threatened by her. Libby knew her secret — if there was one.

She turned toward home. She and Callie had walked as far as the Preserve and Gather Café, where lights illuminated Maxine and Chalice at a table inside. Libby pushed open the door. "You're open?" she asked the woman at the counter.

"Yes, we're open for Halloween. Just til nine. We're closing in half an hour."

"That's all I have in me," Libby said. "Can I get a purple passionflower?"

She sat down with Maxine and Chalice.

"You're not trick-or-treating with your little boy?"

"God, no. I hate it. He's with Kirk. It's a boys' night out."

"We were talking about the other night. The Ouroboros."

Libby admired the way Maxine could say the word like it was just an ordinary thing, not some odd, pagan symbol. "The Ouroboros in particular or the evening?"

"The evening," said Chalice. "What did you think?"

"Hmmm. I hadn't tried to meditate in a long time. I'd rather draw. I find that meditative. I go someplace else when I'm drawing."

"I go into an altered space when I'm playing my cello."

"I used to Sufi dance," said Maxine. "It was better than smoking dope. Now I'm too old to do either."

Boy, that Maxine is a dark horse, Libby thought as she and Callie walked home. That was fun, running into the two of them. What an evening it's been. We left around eight to walk around the block and now it's nearly ten. Haven't seen Brianna in a while. I wonder what she's doing tonight.

When they rounded the entrance to Libby's house, there, as if on cue, was Brianna, sitting on the step. Callie undulated with joy the length of the walkway and porch.

"Hey, stranger! What's going on?"

"Can I stay the night with you?"

"What happened?"

"My stupid mother happened."

Libby unlocked the front door. The girl and the dog curled up on the couch in the front room. Libby rummaged in the kitchen. "Hot chocolate?" she called.

Brianna poked at the marshmallows with a spoon. Libby waited. "I'm working on application forms for college. She wants me to go to a Bible college and I don't want to. She said it wouldn't kill me to fill out the application, and I said yes it would. We screamed at each other for half an hour and I left."

"Where do you want to go?"

"I'm applying to Western and UW, but I don't want to go to either because I want to get as far as possible from her."

"There are schools farther away than Western and UW, if that's your main requirement."

"I want to go to Whitman." Brianna immediately turned red.

"Whitman. I bet you could get in with your grades," Libby said. "But isn't it really expensive?"

"I could get financial aid. Or I could try. I don't see why I shouldn't apply. Or why I should apply to a Bible college when I don't want to go to one."

"Doesn't April's son go to Whitman? Maybe she would be a good person to talk..." Libby paused. "Ah. April's son goes to Whitman."

Brianna attentively massaged Callie, who rolled over in utter ecstasy.

"You like him," Libby said carefully.

"Sort of. Yeah."

"Do you know how he feels about you?"

"We text a lot," Brianna said enigmatically. "He's coming home for Thanksgiving. He wants April to invite me and my mom for dinner."

"I'll be there."

"Really?" Brianna looked up. "Maybe it won't be so bad."

Part III: NOVEMBER

Chapter Fifteen

Kimberly and Rambles overshoot

On the second Saturday in November, the Ouroboros hissed a snaky little laugh in the dark of its hiding place in the Regift Cabinet. It did a self-satisfied stretch, or as much of one as it could within those confines. It curled up with its tail in its mouth and hardened back into Chalice's pottery creation. Tonight was another Night Out.

Chase had the flu. Chalice had stopped short of calling in a hazmat team but hired a cleaning service to sterilize the house while she consulted her herbalist about remedies and Kirk quietly administered 7UP and Flintstone vitamins to their son. Midafternoon she remembered the Ouroboros meeting planned for that evening. She didn't want any fresh injections of God knew what in her newly disinfected home but she didn't want to cancel, either. Chalice knew from rehearsals that you have to keep to a predictable schedule if you want something to work. April and Bob lived just up the alley; it would be easy to move everyone up there. Except that April would balk. So Chalice called Bob.

"Sure, Chalice." Bob looked at his wife, who was massaging Rambles on her lap. "They can all come up here. Just reroute them."

"Who exactly is *all*?" April screwed up her face. Rambles jumped down from her lap and stalked off. "Not the group. I don't want them here."

"Well, I do. It's just one evening."

"Oh, all right. I'll call Kay and make sure she'll take care of ALL the refreshments." She picked up her phone. "As long as all I have to do is just be here."

"Fine. You can be my guest."

"I'll never understand your attachment to this church — hi, Kay? Change of plans."

Kay arrived early, wearing jeans and a patchwork tunic in shades of purple under her puffy coat. Bob helped her unload the trunk of her car. They brought in her giant water heater, a stack of Tupperware, and a large jar filled with an amber liquid.

April was washing supper dishes. "The kitchen is all yours. I need to upgrade my attire to a bra and clean T-shirt."

Kay handed her a hip flask. "It's an Old Fashioned."

April unscrewed the stopper with a grin. She took a small sip. Kay's Old Fashioneds were precise: one teaspoon sugar, splash of Angostura bitters, tiny bit of water, enough Jack Daniel's to make you take it seriously, fill with ice. Kay stopped adding any kind of muddled fruit after a stint at Weight Watchers.

"Umm. Perfect," April said. "Is that what's in the jar?"

"No. Cider." Kay waved her off and busied herself. She poured the cider into the battered old water heater. She scrubbed at a splash on her purple tunic. She hummed "cigarettes and whiskey and wild, wild, women."

Bob ran the vacuum in the living room. He attacked the nest of cat hair on one end of the sofa, then ran the attachment down the sides of his trousers, where little bits of fuzz clung because there'd been a tissue explosion in the last laundry. He collected a stack of books and papers and put them in the computer room.

In the kitchen he found Kay laying out what looked like hors d'oeuvres for a *Sunset* magazine wedding reception: figs wrapped in bacon, cucumbers with cream cheese, lox and capers, a spinach boat and Ritz crackers.

Bob looked speculatively at Kay. He wasn't one to gossip, but he was an historian and as such had a curiosity about people and events. He knew the church was financially strapped. He had to wonder if it involved more than the usual money woes of a small church.

"Kay, what do you know about the church's debt?"

"We're paying bills just barely. The loan for the wing comes due in January." Kay looked at him shrewdly. Men were so easy, she thought. "Kimberly gambles regularly up at Tulalip but I don't think she actually steals anything more than the petty cash from the church. Then she wins it back. It comes and goes like the twenty pounds on my butt."

There was a silence. Bob held out his hands. "How did you know that's what I wanted to know?"

"I'm almost eighty years old. You think I don't know things?"

"No, ma'am, I don't."

"Here." Kay handed him the flask. "Have a slug."

He tipped the flask and had a slug. He poured a finger in a glass and sat at the kitchen table.

"Something else must be going on. Petty cash is just that. Petty."

"I took delivery of a case of wine a few months ago during one of Esme's endless dentist appointments. We wouldn't use that much wine for communion if the church was still standing at the apocalypse."

"Hmmm."

"I think Kimberly's not the only one with a habit."

Kimberly arrived in a tailored beige suit with a stark white blouse and in hose and moderate heels. Around her neck was a tiny cross. Her power attire. She had a giant notepad under her arm, tote bags in her hands, and Victor in tow. He wore a jacket and tie and carried an easel. They came in with identical clerical bon vivant.

"Can I rearrange chairs a little?"

"Sure. Here, I'll help."

"No, that's all right. Victor can do it."

"Then let me take your coat. You look nice."

"I think it's important to dress well when I'm presenting," Kimberly said and immediately regretted it. It made her sound nervous. (It actually made her sound pretentious but that wasn't a word she knew.) She glanced sideways at Bob to see if he noticed, but he was picking a piece of fluff from his trousers. She bit her lip.

Chalice arrived with the Ouroboros. She had meant to get there much earlier so as to cede as little of the floor as possible to Kimberly. Too late. The coffee table where Chalice had meant to assemble the altar had been pushed aside to make room for Kimberly's arrangement of chairs. She was further thrown off by the sight of Victor.

"Let me get a table for the altar," Bob said.

"I'm not sure there's enough room for that tonight," Kimberly interposed.

"Oh, we have to make room for our mascot." He deftly removed a few plants from a columnar plant stand and set it where it gave the altar pride of place without disturbing Kimberly's floor plan.

Chalice whipped the Ouroboros out of its velvet shroud and set it on the stand. The altar towered over the room. Kimberly frowned.

"So this is the famous Ouroboros." Victor studied the sculpture. "A snake eating its own tail."

"I didn't expect to see you here," Chalice said.

"I didn't want to influence the first few meetings."

Chalice fussed at the velvet bedding. "God, they are both insufferable," she thought. Then to the astonishment of everyone present, she pushed her fingers through her hair, pulled up on her head, and flung her arms straight above her head, her face raised toward her hands. She held her position until April and the fragrance of hot spiced cider wafted into the room.

April observed Chalice in this extraordinary pose and noted that Victor was in her living room. She wondered how an Old Fashioned might enhance a mug of cider.

"We're going to need a table for the food." She pulled a series of nesting tables seemingly from out of nowhere.

"I didn't plan to serve food," Kimberly said. She suddenly felt petulant.

Libby and Maxine arrived. Kay came out of the kitchen with the spinach boat. She stood still, her face beaming with anticipation at the sight of Libby, Victor, and Kimberly all in the same room.

A month ago, Libby would have wanted to shrink into the wall. Now she raised her chin. "Hello," she said to no one in particular.

The room went quiet. Rambles stalked in and meowed. April picked up the cat and watched the scene from under lowered lashes. Bob took the spinach boat from Kay and set it silently on a table. Kimberly felt mutinous.

"What's going on?" Chalice finally asked.

No one answered her. The doorbell rang. Wanda and Mrs. Johansen diffused the awkwardness. By the time Sheila arrived — late and with tear-streaked cheeks — April and Bob were passing out mugs of cider and Kay was circulating the room with a tray of bacon-wrapped figs.

Sheila had been expecting a quiet evening. She was upset. For once she thought the frosty politeness of Seattleites would be soothing. But now here they all were acting like normal people. It looked like a cocktail party. She smelled spices. They were nuts about spices here. Cardamom. What was this love affair with cardamom?

Maxine flowed across the room to say hello to Sheila. Privately Maxine had assessed her as someone who was determined to be unhappy, but Maxine had known a lot of people like that. The world was full of them.

Sheila's tear-streaked story was that she had gone to meet someone who had smiled at her on a dating site. They had arranged to meet at the Starbucks at Barnes & Noble in University Village. Sheila sat for an hour in the Starbucks on the corner by the bookstore while her online smiler waited at the Starbucks inside the bookstore, and they had failed to connect. All of this reflected badly on everyone who lived on the entire West Coast. She had made up her mind: she was going to move back home where people behaved like human beings.

"North Carolina?" Maxine asked kindly.

Sheila burst into tears. "South," she sobbed and collapsed onto the sofa that of late had been matted with cat fur.

Wanda meanwhile had cornered Libby, hoping to engage her in conversation about Brianna's college applications. Dissatisfied when Libby didn't appear to have anything useful to say, she sat down next to Mrs. Johansen. The two watched with disapproval at Kay's flirting around the room like a French maid with her tray of hors d'oeuvres.

Kimberly set down her mug of cider, from which she had taken one brief sip. She brushed her hands and positioned herself in front of the chairs. She was about to say something when Chalice clapped her hands.

"Shall we get started?" Chalice asked brightly, coming to stand slightly in front of Kimberly. "I thought we might want to do a little meditation first, to reinforce what we did last time. Then Kimberly has the Main Event. Did anyone bring anything for the altar? No? Well, then, I wonder if we could add a small bowl of saltwater. For purification. April?"

April had just started a mahjong solitaire game on her phone. She started up.

Kay pushed her back down. "I'll do it."

Chalice looked at Victor. "For anyone who wasn't here last time, we did three short sits."

"What's a short sit?" Victor asked. "Is that yoga?"

"No, you're thinking of a pose. Or maybe prana." Chalice preened. Just a little. "A sit is how long you meditate for."

"In a service, I would never expect people to stay quiet for more than thirty seconds." Victor threw down *his* expertise.

"We worked up to three minutes."

"Really, well I think that probably — "

"Let's just get this started," Kimberly cut off her husband. "And over with," she added to herself.

They got through the one-minute sit, and April played her solitaire game.

"You're not being a good guest," Bob murmured.

Finally Kimberly got the floor. Her proposal that they collect a list of behaviors that constituted Godlike behavior was met with a stunned silence. April looked up from her game. Rambles leaped off the couch and left the room.

Kay asked, "Godlike? You mean all full of our own self-importance?"

Kimberly flushed. "I meant *Godly.*"

"Perhaps *Christ-like* would be a more accessible expression," Maxine suggested.

"OK, fine. *Christ*-like."

Kay, amused at Kimberly's posing, could see that she was dead serious. Because she wanted to see what would happen next, she resisted the urge to look at April, who had set down her phone.

Kimberly and Victor lifted Bibles out of the tote bags and passed them around the room. "I've already chosen some verses to get you started." She distributed a three-page handout, on which everyone could see the fruits of her recent retreat.

Kay read a few lines and snorted. "What is this really about, Kimberly?" she asked.

"What do you mean?"

"Well, here's one: 'Don't be flip with the sacred.' Who is being flip with the sacred? If this is about that calendar page you walked in on, why don't you just say so?"

"What calendar?" asked Mrs. Johansen.

"'You shall not covet your neighbor's house,'" read April over Bob's shoulder. "What's that doing there? Who's coveting a house?"

"It's there because it's one of the Ten Commandments." Kimberly actually didn't know why it was there. Had Victor added it?

Victor cleared his throat. "If I may," he began before changing into what he imagined was a sympathetic tone. "April, you know I think that your labyrinth is beautiful, but weren't you coveting my idea?"

April snorted. "First of all, Victor," she said, "I am not one of your church flunkies." She pushed away Bob's constraining hand. "Secondly, I don't think you can apply the concept of covet to an idea. Wouldn't you have to *have* a labyrinth for me to covet it, and who uses the word *covet*, anyway?"

"And Chalice," Victor moved on smoothly because he was in over his head and he knew it. "You began this group without consulting me or availing yourself of my help. What was that about?"

"It's about someone who doesn't know what a sit is," Chalice flushed. "And what about you, interrupting my rehearsals and interfering in my music?"

Kimberly was more successful in her effort to shut Victor up than Bob had been with April. In fact, Kimberly couldn't be more constraining than if she had picked Victor up like a plank of wood and nailed him to a house frame. She pinned him with the fiercest look in her repertoire. He sat down.

Kay was another matter. She was a champion in this division. Plus she had about twenty-five years more experience. She rattled the handout. "'You were bought at a price. Don't be enslaved by the world,'" she read. "Like with gambling, Kimberly?"

Kimberly froze.

Victor looked at Kay "What do you mean?"

"You don't know?"

"Know what?"

"What calendar?" Mrs. Johansen asked.

"Here's one that says it all," Bob said quickly. "'Love justice and walk humbly with your god.'"

Rambles walked humbly into the room. He studied everyone in turn, his nose twitching.

Kimberly referred everyone to the third page of her handout, which contained the whole of Psalm 139 and ending with the words: "Search me, God, and know my heart; test me and know my anxious thoughts. See if there is any offensive way in me and lead me in the way everlasting."

"Maybe if we just focus on that last part," she said. "Maybe this was too much at once."

"I'll say," Kay persisted. "Psalm 139. Isn't that the one abortion protesters trot out all the time? Kimberly, do you have any actual experience with a woman who has undergone an abortion, or is it all academic with you?"

April had gone back to her mahjong solitaire game but although she was staring at her phone, she didn't see it. What had gotten into Kay? She was afraid to look up.

Rambles eyed the distance from his place on the floor to the top of the column that usually had a plant on it. He gathered his energies and jumped. Too late, he learned the column wasn't built to sustain the impact of a flying cat. His hind feet pushed back, the column rocked, and the Ouroboros crashed to the floor, breaking into pieces at Kimberly's feet. The bowl of saltwater emptied itself onto Kimberly's medium-heeled beige pumps. Rambles scrambled onto the closest solid object, the piano. He landed on octave three, leaped off, and shot out of the room.

Chalice jumped up with a cry. She pushed Kimberly out of the way and crouched to collect pieces of the snake. Bob moved the plant stand and knelt on the floor to help. Chalice was seething. Her spirituality group had been hijacked. The Ouroboros that she communed with was broken. She'd left her aspen drops at home.

"I'll get a broom." Bob went through the kitchen where Rambles was unconcernedly munching kibble from his bowl. "How can things go wrong so quickly?" he heard someone ask and then realized it was him.

"It may be that nothing has gone wrong," said Maxine.

Rambles came out of the kitchen and looked with interest at the pile of pottery Chalice had transferred to a nesting table. He jumped up to sniff at the recently deceased snake, then, as if to punctuate his earlier part in its death, he vomited up a hairball with the kibble he had just ingested.

"Hard to make that argument now," April murmured.

They all agreed to call it a night. Kimberly said she would pledge to meditate on the end of Psalm 139 and made a stiff-necked plea for everyone to do the same. Everyone said, "yeah, yeah," though no one, in fact, planned to give it another thought.

"What calendar were they talking about?" Mrs. Johansen asked no one in particular as they filed out into the dark.

Chapter Sixteen

Kimberly walks a labyrinth, she and Victor gang up on Chalice

The Ouroboros group was underrepresented at church the next day. Chalice wasn't there because the choir wasn't singing. Sheila wasn't there because she had written off the entire Pacific Northwest and was busy with her plans to get the hell out of Dodge. Bob wasn't there because he and April were picking their son Nicholas up from the airport. Of course April wouldn't be caught dead at a service unless something remarkably interesting was going on and one could hardly top the previous night for pure human interest.

Kay, Wanda, and Mrs. Johansen were there. Kimberly noted the three with approval, except for Kay. Imagine Kay taking her on like that! Kimberly allowed she might have gotten a little carried away with herself. She did that when she knew she was right. It was her one failing.

She turned off Victor's sermon (she knew it, she had edited it) and reviewed recent events.

The car ride home from the Marches' was as ominous as if they'd left the Bates Motel. Kimberly's knives were out but Victor was vacant as a room. If she didn't mention the subjects of gambling and abortion, she knew they wouldn't register with him. They would linger in a preregistration line at an office that was closed.

Things had been frosty ever since the weekend when the extended family of squirrels had crashed Luther Memorial's youth group retreat. Kimberly had ordered Victor to call a proper pest control business.

"Call a trapper," she had said at the door to his home office, then went into the front room to read an old issue of *Bible and Belief*.

She heard Victor calling several pest control services before it finally dawned on him that he needed a trapper. Then he called a trapper.

"Are the squirrels gone?" she asked in the car on the short ride home from Ouroboros, wanting to be the first to say something so as to appear the least petty and this being the least inflammatory subject she could think of.

"They finished the cleaning up today."

"I'm going to bed," she said when they got home.

Sunday morning, Kimberly greeted people at the church door. She listened with a clergy wife's glazed attention to the joys and concerns of the congregation while watching for Mr. and Mrs. Fred Johansen II. She needed to quell Muffy's curiosity about the calendar.

But when she finally caught up with Mrs. Johansen at the coffee hour, Kay had gotten to her first. "Kay said she and Bob's wife, what's her name, May or June or something, were making a calendar for a fund-raiser for the church. I think it's a marvelous idea. People get tired of rummage sales."

Kimberly hesitated.

"She said the subject of the calendar was about humor in the church, which I thought a little odd because I don't see what's funny about the Lord's House, but she said there would be photos of gardens and flowers, which would be lovely."

Kimberly decided to leave it at that.

Muffy persisted. "Kay had a photo of herself behind the most gorgeous purple hydrangea. She was clearly naked but I thought it was quite tastefully done. Our Gwen took the photo. You know," she lowered her voice conspiratorially, "Fred is an amateur photographer. He used to take…" She mouthed, "… naked pictures of me!"

Kimberly sat down heavily on a cold folding chair.

"But it was a long time ago," Muffy tittered like the young woman she once was and swanned off to speak to Gwen, who was tottering on her spike heels by the coffee urn and eating pineapple-banana bread.

Kimberly bent down to pick up a chunk of coffee-hour pastry of indeterminate age and found herself nose to nose with Marvin. She dropped the pastry back onto the floor for the dog to hoover up and sat up with a ready smile for Corinne, who couldn't be far behind. Corinne reeled in Marvin's leash as she closed in on Kimberly and sat down with a cackle at the sight of her dog begging for more food.

"When can we go to the casino again?" she asked.

Kimberly laughed and casually scanned the room. From the north, a pair of beige Naturalizers clumped toward her. In one efficient move of her neck, she frowned, shook her head slightly at Corinne, and smiled up at Wanda. Wanda pulled up a chair.

"I wanted to ask you something. Is there some time I could see you? Hi, Corinne. It's about Brianna. She's been asking questions about," she said sotto voce, "abortion, and I'm worried she might be," she now whispered, "pregnant."

Kimberly's smile froze.

"I've had an abortion," volunteered Corinne. "What does she want to know?"

"Can you come by later this afternoon?" Kimberly stood up and smoothed her skirt. "I've got to grab um, Mrs.…" She fled through the kitchen and into the new wing.

In the round room, Kimberly sat on a folding chair, chewed her lip, and looked at the plastic labyrinth anchored onto the floor with weights. She wondered if it would even work, whatever that meant exactly. Wouldn't it rip after a dozen people had trampled it? She didn't see the point of it.

She got up and entered the labyrinth, slowly tracing its circuits. At the center, she stopped and looked at the loop-backs and patterns she had walked. She suddenly gasped, pressed her hands to her mouth, and stared at nothing for a good long time. She had decided something. She was going back to school. She was going to get her Doctor of Divinity. Instead of The Minister's Wife, she would become The Minister.

From the center, she cut across the plastic labyrinth. She straightened out a wrinkle, moved one of the weights, and looked at the circle on the floor. She still didn't see the point of it.

The destruction of her Ouroboros necessitated Chalice doing a complete mind and body cleanse, which was accomplished by an all-day retreat with her Healer and two follow-up sessions. This was done in tandem with her re-embarking on her musical studies. The maestro up north had agreed to take her on, and this had thrilled Chalice to the ends of the earth.

It was a long commute to her cello lessons, though not quite to the ends of the earth. Marysville, known for the famous pies of its Village Café, was a forty-minute drive to the north of Seattle. The drive allowed Chalice time to commune with herself and to stop at the Village Café. There was no refined sugar in the Martin home so Chalice had to get hers on the outside. With a twice weekly piece of pie, Chalice was on track to sample all twenty-seven of its different kinds of pies before her first orchestra audition in February.

The other great Marysville attraction, though it didn't attract Chalice, was the Tulalip Resort casino.

After one particularly intense lesson, Chalice barely had time to bolt a piece of warm apple pie à la mode in the Village Café before hurrying back to Seattle for a meeting with Victor. He had been vague about its purpose but alluded to something about the Christmas pageant and to Chalice being a mom. She pulled into her driveway. Kirk and Chase were at Tae Kwon Do. She carefully unloaded her cello and secured it in its hallowed corner in her dining room. Then she fortified herself with drops and puffed up the alley to the church.

Both Victor's Cadillac and Kimberly's Legacy were parked behind the church. In Victor's office, Kimberly was ensconced in a chair looking comfortable and, Chalice thought, a little smug. Her antennae were immediately out though a bit tied up in the twinings of a theme from Bach she had worked on for two hours earlier in the day. Also by the apple pie (à la mode). Her eyes narrowed but she just managed to stop herself from demanding, "What are you doing here?"

"Hello, Chalice," Kimberly said smoothly. "It's good to see you after the other night. I'm sorry about your snake."

That marked the extent of Chalice's forbearance. "What are you doing here?" she demanded.

Victor offered her a chair. "I asked her to be here. We were wondering if we might want to make some adjustments to your job description."

"What does Kimberly have to do with my job description?"

"I asked her to be here because — "

"Because you're afraid of me?"

"No, because you're afraid of me."

"I'm not afraid of you, Victor. I would be glad to review my job description. And *yours* if it comes to that. I'm tired of your interference in the music."

"I do have some experience, Chalice."

"No, you don't." Chalice, coming from two hours on three lines of Bach, was scornful.

Kimberly gave her husband A Look.

"But you. *You* are a real professional," Victor said magnanimously.

"A *scrupulous* professional," Kimberly added. "We're so lucky to have you."

"I still don't see why she is here," the scrupulous professional addressed herself to the principal and ignored the supernumerary.

"When you told me you wanted to watch Chase in the Christmas pageant rather than participate in it yourself, I wondered if maybe you want to devote more time to being a mother."

"What business is that of yours?"

"I'm concerned about everyone in the church."

Chalice looked at him with distaste. He actually seemed to puff up. "I don't need you to be concerned about me," she said. "I'm fine."

Kimberly leaned forward and spoke gently. "Chalice, you know, Victor and I have a daughter we never see, who lives as far away as she can from us. We tried to be involved in her life but we lost her. She had such qualities. She could have done something beautiful for God. I regret every day that I didn't spend with her."

Chalice rolled her eyes. "I don't see what your experience with your daughter has to do with my job at this church."

"I saw you at the pie café in Marysville last week. It was after school and I wondered why you weren't with Chase."

Sugar, Bach, and cello vibrations were no match for a few aspen drops. Chalice stood up and reeled on her feet. "Are you *spying* on me?"

"No, no, no, of course not. I just happened to be there."

"And so did I just happen to be there. Do you hear me asking you what *you* were doing there? Should I wonder why you aren't down here where your congregation is?"

Chalice was fully loaded and ready to spit fire, saliva, and Mystifyx-87. She was taken aback when Kimberly suddenly sat back in her chair and looked, well, a little frightened. So she turned on Victor.

"What, are you going to fire me for not being a good enough mother?"

"Chalice, c'mon," he laughed uncomfortably.

"Then stay the hell out of my life."

Chalice marched out the door with as much dignity as she could scrape up. Once in the alley, she pressed her hands to her cheeks. She moved away from the door and breathed (singing breaths) until she stopped shaking. Chalice saw April's car pull into her parking strip across the street. The car door slammed. April greeted the cat.

Chalice walked to the top of the alley and crossed the street.

April, pulling a tray of winter cabbage from the back of her Explorer, looked up. "You look gone to seed. If you've been at the church, I'm not surprised you bolted." She laughed at her own joke.

"Can I come in for a minute? I can't go home yet."

"Let's go through the sunroom so I can put these down."

Chalice held the tray of plants while April unlocked the sliding glass door. "The strangest thing just happened."

April took the tray. "Yeah? What's that?" She settled the plants in the weak November light.

"Kimberly saw me at the pie café in Marysville, so she and Victor think I'm not being a good enough mother."

"He got Kimberly over there to gang up on you? My God, those two. Wait. Kimberly saw you in Marysville?" April chuckled. "You know what she was doing up there, don't you?"

"No."

"She goes up to the casino at Tulalip. She probably thought you were doing the same thing."

"Kimberly?"

"Yes."

"She gambles?"

"Why do you think all the petty cash keeps disappearing?"

"Does Victor know?"

"I don't know. I doubt it. Listen, Chalice. This has nothing to do with you. She saw you up there and she's worried that you know why she was there. Now you've got something on her. Call her bluff."

Chalice didn't know what that meant. She didn't want to have anything on anyone. "I just want to be left alone."

"I hear that."

"Oh, I'm sorry. You just got home, you have things to do."

"No, that's not what I meant. All I want in the whole world is to just be in my garden. I imagine you're that way with your music."

"Well, actually, that's what I was doing in Marysville. I'm studying cello again and I'm getting ready to audition."

"Good for you. Listen, Chase has two parents. It's not going to help him to be raised by one with an unlived life."

Chalice opened the sliding door. "Thanks, April."

"My pleasure. And Chalice, don't underestimate the power in having something over Kimberly."

Chapter Seventeen

The Marches host Thanksgiving

"Pop some spirits of Ouroboros into this," April said, holding out a pie shell.

Nicholas, stirring apples and flour in a bowl, sighed. "Explain again to me why that is funny."

"It's not funny, really. It's sad."

"I'll say."

April smiled. It was lovely to have him home.

"What time are the Carpenters coming?"

April glanced at her son. "I told them any time after two but we won't eat til four. My friend Libby is coming, too."

Bob came into the kitchen and found an apron to tie on. "Let's get this bird in the oven so we can be off on our bikes."

April rolled out a top crust for the pie while Nicholas drained the brined turkey and Bob set out the roasting pan. This was the tradition on Thanksgiving morning: the whole family participated in making the meal or else they got grilled cheese sandwiches. April had been adamant that Nicholas learn to cook when he was growing up, and he didn't get out of lending a hand just because he was home from college. Nicholas knew how to roast a turkey. He had handled the entire operation his senior year of high school.

Rambles sauntered in and jumped in the sink. Nicholas ran some water.

"What's everyone bringing?" he asked.

"Wanda said she would bring flan, one of her Mexican memories, and Libby is bringing cranberries and rolls."

"Brianna is bringing *ponche*," Nicholas pronounced the Spanish carefully.

"You don't say?"

"I told her if I am doing the turkey, she has to make something, too."

April paused with the dough poised above the pie. Bob stopped stirring the stuffing. Rambles jumped down. The water continued to run.

"When did you talk to Brianna?"

"We text," Nicholas said.

April and Bob exchanged glances.

April turned off the water. "And what exactly is *ponche*?"

"Bri describes it as a hot fruit punch that you can float things in, like pieces of sugarcane or guava."

"*Bri*," April mouthed to Bob.

The three worked in silence until the turkey was in the oven and the pie and stuffing were waiting in line.

"Let's go for this ride, then," Nicholas said. "Mom?"

"What? I'm not going."

He jerked a thumb at the jackets, caps, and one bra hanging on the pantry hooks.

"Oh, right." April grabbed the bra and shoved it in the pocket of her bathrobe. "See you later. Come on, Rambles. You and I are going to pick the centerpiece."

The March men left for their ride. April got dressed and went into her garden with Rambles and her secateurs. The assembled centerpiece was of baby pumpkins and Indian corn on a bed of autumn leaves and adorned with rosemary, tiny pine cones, and a few late roses, preserved in their bloom by the cold.

Libby and Callie arrived shortly after noon. The two women curled up on a couch in the family room for a draught of cider and a good natter about the Ouroboros debacle. Rambles stationed himself by the oven door but padded in every few minutes to disapprove of Callie, sleeping on the rug by the wood stove.

"I felt a little sorry for Kimberly. People expect so much of a pastor's wife," Libby said. "It's like being a regular woman times a hundred. Kimberly's problem is that she tries to live up to her own inhuman standards. Then she imagines that no one sees right through her."

"You got all that from the other night?"

"I recognize the type. I used to be like that, only I didn't have Kimberly's need to control. I would do anything to not have to endure criticism. I really hated being married," she concluded, as though the two were inseparable.

April was silent. She wasn't particularly reflective. She liked that Libby was.

"You and Bob seemed to have made it work."

"Luck of the draw, really. We lived together for five years before we got married, and I told him right from the start that I wasn't doing anything for him that an able-bodied adult couldn't do for himself. We raised Nicholas to be an able-bodied person. He was doing his own laundry when he was ten years old."

"I'm looking forward to meeting him."

"I think he and Brianna have a little thing."

"Did he tell you about that?"

"You know?"

"Brianna told me. She spent the night a few weeks ago—Halloween, actually. She and her mother had had a fight about colleges. She wants to apply to Whitman, but Wanda wants her to go to a Bible college."

"You know Victor and Kimberly have a daughter who lives on the east coast and never speaks to them? They tried to force her to go to a Bible College. I imagine by now she has as many piercings as Brianna. And more tattoos." April drained her mug. "Should be interesting today."

Nicholas was basting the turkey when Wanda and Brianna arrived. Brianna grinned shyly and Wanda said, "My goodness."

"C'mon, Bri," he said, untying his dark blue apron imprinted with "Whitman College" in gold lettering. "Let's go walk the labyrinth."

"C'mon, Bri, let's get away from the adults," Bob said as the four of them watched through the kitchen window. "Let's go sit in the other room. They're going to be out there a good long while."

Wanda bunched up her forehead. "Are you okay with them?" she asked nervously.

"Of course," April said. "They're fine. Just let's give them space."

Wanda was an obstruction to talking about anything related to the church so April was glad Libby had come early. It was *why* Libby had come early. Bob engaged Wanda in talk about Mexico and Aztec ruins. Then Wanda told some interesting stories from her work as a paralegal. Libby told with relish the tale of being jilted by her now ex-husband for someone named Chantal LeBec. Wanda appeared fascinated with her insouciance. Even April was surprised. Her friend had come a long way in the few months she had known her.

Brianna and Nicholas reentered the house smelling of marijuana. April inserted herself between the two young people — giving them A Look — and Wanda. The entire party assembled in the kitchen to witness Nicholas carving the turkey, the fragrance of which masked all other odors.

"It's not that big a deal," Nicholas said. "Stop staring."

During dinner, April was amused to see Wanda visibly relax when Nicholas behaved like a normal human being, not someone likely to jump her daughter's bones. Wanda surprised everyone by relating that her childhood family always had pickled asparagus at Thanksgiving, and there was a competition for who made the first asparagus pee. This led to talk of family holiday traditions.

"We have a tradition to which you are all invited," Bob said. "Our Thanksgiving Day Holly Caper: after dark and before the pie, we go to the cemetery next door and collect a few bags of holly."

"I like having holly in the house for Christmas," April explained. "But I won't have a holly tree in my yard. It hogs sunlight."

"Is that legal?" Wanda bunched up her forehead.

Brianna sighed. "Of course not, Mom."

"Crown Hill Cemetery has some lovely holly trees," April said. "They're understaffed there and don't have the time or expertise to shape them, so we're really doing them a favor."

She watched with satisfaction as Wanda's brow smoothed. Her face finally broke into a smile and she shook her head at April. "I'll go," she said.

Brianna gave April a bear-hug while everyone got their coats. "Thank you," she whispered.

"You're welcome," April whispered back. Then she added, "Other things aren't legal."

After the Holly Caper, after the pumpkin pie and the apple pie and the cranberry pie and the flan, Wanda, Libby and Callie went home. Bob put his feet up. Brianna and Nicholas cleared the table and washed the dishes. April put on her hunter-green puffy coat and her miner's light. She was going to walk her labyrinth.

"Do you have any left?" she asked Nicholas.

He fished in his pocket and pulled out a plastic bag with a joint and matchbook inside. "Here you go."

April took it out into the cold night.

Part IV: DECEMBER

Chapter Eighteen

The Ouroboros begins eating its new tail

The Ouroboros had died with its smirk on. After the November meeting, the broken sculpture was interred in velvet in the back of the Regift Cabinet. Chalice had wanted to chuck it in the trash, but Maxine had walked her home and talked her into a symbolic burial.

"Leave it for the next meeting."

"There's not going to be another meeting."

"But that would interrupt the cycle at its most powerful point. The pottery Ouroboros is broken. It's eaten its own head. It's dead. Don't you want to see what it's given birth to? Isn't that the point of the symbol?"

Maxine led the December Ouroboros. Chalice hadn't wanted to. Actually Maxine hadn't wanted to either; she was in a different phase of her life. But she roused herself and did some communing of her own before walking the few blocks to the Martin home, where she helped Kay unload her Tupperware from the back of her car.

"Let's take these in through the kitchen," Kay said. "It's like a morgue in the front room."

They carried everything through the back door into the kitchen, which Chalice had ceded to Kay without so much as a sigh. Kay pushed aside the Mystifix-87 and a small battalion of supplements, pushed up her sweater sleeves, and set to work. Maxine carried on into the front room, where Chalice was in black from head to toe, skull earrings dangling from her ear-lobes.

Maxine stifled a chuckle. "Very apt, Chalice. Now where is the Ourobouros?"

She fit the chunks of pottery back into the snake form and let them fall away into a circle of broken pieces. Thirty minutes later, most of the group was assembled and looking bleakly at the reminder of last month's meeting. A reading of the minutes could not have been more effective. Even Mrs. Johansen thought so but never would have said it out loud.

Victor and Kimberly both looked subdued. For once neither of them had a desire to take charge. Libby itched to get her fingers on some charcoal and drawing paper to do studies of the faces in the room. Chinking and rustling sounds from the kitchen punctuated the silence.

"I feel like I've been called to the principal's office," Bob said.

April looked up from her phone. "It was my cat who broke it. I take full responsibility if that's what's needed." If that's what will get this over with, she added to herself.

"Maybe a small bowl of saltwater would help," Wanda ventured. "For purification."

To everyone's astonishment, Maxine burst out laughing. "I think you're all missing the point. This isn't a wake. Well, okay, maybe it is, but a wake is a celebration of life as much as a recognition of death. That's the message of the Ouroboros. I thought perhaps we could talk about life. Our lives. I don't really know any of you. What's ahead for you in the new year?"

Kay banged through the kitchen door with a plate of frosted sugar cookies: angels with boobs, reindeer with testicles, erotic elves, and a few chaste snowmen. She took drink orders and hied back to the kitchen.

"Brianna got early acceptance at Whitman College — with a scholarship, so we can just swing the tuition!" Wanda piped up.

At this April looked up. She and Bob chorused their enthusiasm.

"I'm going to train for this summer's Seattle to Portland ride," Bob said. "Maybe after I recover, I'll ride Seattle to Walla Walla and embarrass both kids!"

"What's happening with the calendar I've been hearing so much about?" This was a provocation. Maxine had managed in the past four months to learn everything there was to know about the calendar.

Libby took this one. "I'm designing it. And I've gotten a contract with a national card and stationery company for my illustrations. Maybe when this calendar gets finished, we'll already have a publisher for it."

Kay, relaying drinks into the room, looked at Kimberly and Victor, still sitting quietly.

"What's going on with you two?" she asked. This, too, was a provocation.

"What? Nothing."

"Oh, please. You look like you're trying to hatch something."

Kimberly broke open as wide a smile as anyone had seen on her in recent memory. Maybe ever. The group pulled away from her, ever so slightly. This was more unnerving than Kimberly bearing down on a photography session or, in Victor's case, with a knife in her hands.

"Well, actually, I've made a decision. I'm going back to school to get my Doctor of Divinity."

Kay sat down. "Really? Now that is a surprise."

Victor gazed dispassionately at a reindeer testicle.

"What does that mean for Crown Hill Comm?"

"Nothing so far as my plans go. But there may be other changes at the church."

"Oh?"

At this Kimberly shut down. Victor continued studying the cookies.

"If I may," Mrs. Johansen spoke up.

No one told her she mayn't.

"Fred has been going over the books. Unless we can get some help from the Greater Seattle Church Conference, we aren't going to meet the balloon payment on the loan we took out to build the wing. As you probably know, the wing project hasn't worked out quite as we hoped it would. In addition, there are some unexplained expenditures. Given all that, I doubt the Conference is going to want to help us out."

"So we're going to default? Will a bank repossess a church?"

"We still don't know what will happen."

"How big were the unexplained expenditures?" Kay asked.

"We don't need to go into the details here." Kimberly dived-bombed.

Kimberly had promised Victor that if she could announce her big news, she would protect what they both imagined was the secret of his unauthorized wine purchases. Now she cast wildly about for a way to change the subject.

"Libby, I ran into someone who knew you and your ex," Kimberly said. "Sounds like a painful experience."

This was heavy-handed, not to mention thuggish, even for Kimberly, but it did the trick. It diverted the conversation.

Libby raised her chin and narrowed her eyes. "I seem to have a pattern with men who leave me without saying goodbye. I will say this for Roger, he didn't leave me pregnant."

"My goodness, why would you say that to Kimberly?" Mrs. Johansen's voice faltered. "Like that."

"My husband left me, too." Wanda had never felt so normal. "With a toddler. Where is your child now, Libby?"

"It's not. I had…it didn't work out. Kimberly and I met in the women's clinic."

The two women sat back silently, gazing at nothing, arms folded. The smirk on the dead Ouroboros looked downright nasty. Maxine sighed. This was why she didn't care for groups. Kay sparkled. This was why she did.

"These are private matters between the people involved and not the business of the group as a whole," Maxine interposed. "Chalice, you've been quiet all evening. What are your plans for the new year?"

"I'm studying cello again and plan to audition for an orchestra chair," Chalice said. The power of the Ouroboros caused Chalice to hear herself say, "And I'm resigning from my position at the church effective the first of the year."

The head of the Ouroboros dislodged itself from another chunk of pottery, rocked back and forth, and fell with a clunk on its side.

Chapter Nineteen

Christmas lights up Crown Hill Community Church

Chalice went up to the church the Saturday before the children's Christmas pageant. The sanctuary had gone pink. Inside, Kay and her son Jerry were throwing swag around the nave. They had turned on the lights of the Christmas tree that stood to the left of the pulpit and had draped a number of the bulbs with pastel tulle.

"It's the third week of Advent. We can finally change the color from that dark blue," Kay said. "We're getting rid of the gloom."

"And the decorum," Jerry laughed. Beside him stood the naked lady statue. The fat, cupid-looking baby sprawled across the top of the piano. "Tell us the blocking for the pageant."

"Don't ask me," Chalice said. "It's Victor's pageant. Jeff is playing for it. All the choir does tomorrow is sing a short prelude to the service."

She sat in a front pew and watched Kay and Jerry mug with the statues. There was something soothing about their antics, shudderingly different than Kimberly's dispensations of God-like Behavior. Jeff arrived. He turned on the organ and played the beginning of Bach's *Toccata and Fugue in D minor*. Kay and

Jerry did fantastical poses to its flamboyant phrases. Jeff played the entire prelude and fugue and Chalice joined the interpretive dance. They all clapped.

"I've had the most scathingly brilliant idea!" Chalice said suddenly. "For your calendar. Set up a nativity scene with a baby and two mothers. Mary and Josephine."

"Jesus has two mommies," Jerry said. "I like it. I suppose that under the circumstances, Joseph didn't have to be all that virile."

"I'm calling Gwen. Let's see if we can get her over here to take the picture," said Kay.

"I'll go see if April will play Josephine," said Chalice.

By the end of Saturday the front of the church was a study in pink with the odd twinkle of green here and there. At the foot of the nave, a fat cupid lolled in a manger of hay mixed with tutti-frutti packing straw. The naked lady had been transformed into an angel, but she appeared to be leaning against the piano like a cabaret singer.

April had stamped across the street in work gloves, muddy wellies, and dirt-stained jeans to play Josephine. Gwen was bribed with a batch of Jeff's hot buttered rum to come with her camera and computer.

"There's December's calendar page," Kay said as they all admired Gwen's work with Photoshop.

When Chalice walked into the church on Sunday morning, the sanctuary was swarming with children in bathrobes and beards made from fuzzy toilet-tank covers. An eight-year-old angel in T-shirt and corduroy pants flew importantly about, fussing with her wings and halo. Whining that it itched, Chase was pulling at the beard that Kirk was trying to fasten.

"Chasie, you'll make a great shepherd."

"I don't want to be a shepherd. I want to be a cowherd."

"Oh, I'm sorry, I meant cowherd. You'll be a great cowherd."

"No, I won't." He burst into tears and Chalice drifted away, leaving Kirk to manage.

She went to the piano. The tableaux looked less pink and much less provocative. Kimberly must have blown through and cleared out anything imaginative. Chalice read through the overly edited bulletin that Victor always left for her. He had her at the piano during the pageant. Well, he could forget about that. She wouldn't do it.

"Oh, Chalice." Victor fussed down the side aisle and stepped over two cows and a rock. "There's been a slight change. I will need you to play this part during the pageant." He stabbed at a place in the bulletin he had underlined three times in red, circled, and then highlighted. "Because Jeff will be in the back on the bells and can't be at the piano in time for his cue."

"No."

"Excuse me?"

"No. I said I wanted to watch Chase. Wasn't that the whole point of your little ambush the other week? I'm sorry, but playing for your pageant would just take too much out of me. I'm not up for this."

Victor laughed awkwardly.

"I'm not kidding!" She thought she had just raised her voice, but apparently she had screamed.

Jeff slid out of the organ bench and nipped across the platform. Kirk rushed over, abandoning Chase and another child to fence with staves in proximity of three elderly women and a man in a wheelchair. Kimberly loped down the center aisle, kicking straw and toilet tank covers out of her way.

"Do you realize this man is asking me to take time away from being a mother to play three measures in his miserable little pageant?" Chalice yelled to no one in particular.

Kirk inserted himself between Chalice and the oncoming Kimberly. Jeff declared there was plenty of time for him to get back to the piano after the bells. Kirk ushered Chalice to a front pew, where Chase was about to put out the eye of the man in the wheelchair. He put one arm around his wife and with the other grabbed the staff from his son.

The hall went silent except for yells from a thwarted Chase and one of the elderly women, who was deaf and kept asking what had happened. Out of the corner of her eye, Chalice could see Kimberly managing the storm and directing the whirlwind. She sat with her family until she felt calmer.

Victor and Jeff were arguing.

"But if she's incapable — "

"She's perfectly capable and she'll be fine if you will just leave her alone. You do understand that you have done nothing but undermine her the past four months."

"I? How? I've done everything I could to be supportive of her."

"Trust me, you haven't. But there's no time to get into that now. It's fifteen minutes til showtime — "

"I hate that expression."

"Yes, I know, that's why I said it. Now go get your boas on."

"They are surplices — "

Jeff gave him a push and Victor stumbled down the center aisle.

Jeff sat down with Chalice and Kirk.

"Thank you," Chalice said.

"It's nothing," Jeff said. "Well, actually it is. Take comfort in knowing that musicians have always been treated badly. My grandmother had an expression: 'Ever was.' C'mon, get up. The show must go on. You know how critical to the entire Christmas season your thirty-second choir round is."

It took the full week after the children's pageant to transform Crown Hill Comm into an old-world, fairy-tale church for Christmas. Kay and Jerry practically encamped in the church for the week and conscripted an army of Christian soldiers to decorate.

On Monday evening there was a wind storm; the following morning, April and Kay gathered all the fallen evergreen boughs in the cemetery. Two nights later, they did another Holly Caper and cut three grocery bags of holly.

Danny, the Johansen's grandson and owner of High Noon Pest Control, came mysteriously into twenty-three poinsettias, which he smuggled into the church on Wednesday. No one asked any questions. Kay and Jerry arranged them around the sanctuary like Easter eggs hiding in plain sight.

Corinne and Marvin brought some odd tinsel-like substance Corinne had found at a salvage shop. She thought she could sew strands onto the pillow lumps to make them into festive pillow lumps. This took her the better part of two days.

Bob March and Nicholas, home from Whitman, set up a second Christmas tree in the narthex. Kirk, Chase, and other children from the church decorated it with ornaments they had been making all month. While the adults had sat through the seemingly interminable Advent services, the kids pasted colored macaroni on paper circles and fashioned stars out of dough they weren't supposed to eat. There was more than one incident of diarrhea during a morning service in December.

The Christmas tree in the nave faced the sanctuary: with red balls and white lights against its evergreen boughs, it was stunning in its simplicity. But on the backside that brushed against Jeff at the organ, Kay hung a few erotic ornaments.

Out came the blood-red swag and the lengths of velvet as green as Scarlett O'Hara's dress. They decked the pews and windows as well as the nave. They positioned the naked lady and the fat cupid in provocative positions, knowing that by the time Kimberly had "corrected" things, the display would be just right.

Finally Kay set out the candles: the red pillars that stood on the organ, piano, altar, and in the windows. She got out the small white tapers with their drip shields for the candlelight service on Christmas Eve. When the candles were lit and the church was warm, the fragrance of the evergreen would rise through the hall. Chalice could have told them the scent of evergreen was a remedy for chaos and confusion. The church could have benefited from it sooner.

On Thursday evening, while Corinne was sewing the last of the tinsel on the pillow lumps, Chalice and Jeff rehearsed the choir for the lessons and carols service. There was one simple anthem by John Rutter, not, it hardly need be said, "There Shall a Star Come out of Jacob." The choir had to be marginally more familiar than the congregation with the second and third verses of the carols, so they sang through the familiar old songs, which gave everyone a warm feeling. They rehearsed the *pièce de résistance*: the singing of "Silent Night." Brianna and Amanda were to sign the words and everyone in the sanctuary would hold a lit candle.

The full choir was there, as well as Nicholas, who sang bass along with Susan Moore and Monty McDougal. When they practiced the blocking for the girls to sign "Silent Night," Brianna had an attack of adolescence because Nicholas was there, but she said she would be fine on Christmas Eve.

Bob leaned across the tenor section and murmured to his son, "The March men certainly have an effect on the women."

"Stop it." Nicholas reddened under his urbane, collegiate persona.

Victor tried to crash the rehearsal with a few suggestions. Chalice refused to discuss them. Jeff told Victor that he would talk the program through with him later. Victor protested but Jeff insisted.

"You're going to inflame things and you know it."

"Is she still — ?"

"Of course, she's still."

"But it's Christmas. We need to all make an effort."

"Chalice is making more of an effort than you know."

Victor went home to the other woman who was making an effort and who had no hesitancy in telling him how much.

They've always done a good Christmas at Crown Hill Community Church. The quarrels and pettiness of the year are usually tabled although this particular year presented more of a challenge than usual; one heard the odd remark that they might not make it to heavenly peace this time.

That year brought the first white Christmas in anyone's recent memory. Seattle snows tended to come after the first of the year, if at all. A city of five hills and three snowplows, it shuts down after only a few inches of snow. People leave work early if they see a snowflake at noon.

On the solstice, an arctic blast blew in a blizzard that dumped several feet of snow on the five hills, less in the crevices. Inches of compacted ice covered the main roads, though most people couldn't even get to the main roads. Everyone was encouraged to stay home and do jigsaw puzzles — difficult when half the city was without electricity. Plumbers did a brisk business attending to burst pipes. Danny Johansen became a temporary plumber, leaving his card for High Noon Pest Control with all his new customers.

Crown Hill had not had a power outage in forty-five years and the record held. The March home stayed warm and well-lit. April insulated precious garden plants with burlap and cardboard. Libby and Callie pushed through the drifts to visit in the afternoons when a bright sun glinted the snow. Down the alley from the church, Chalice and Kirk had their solstice ritual (Chalice's invention) without interference from the elements, although Chalice would have celebrated such interference as a visitation, the meaning of which to be decided later.

Crown Hill Comm did not alter its plans for its midnight service on Christmas Eve. The ostensible reasoning was that the streets were no less dark and icy at five o'clock than they were at eleven. But the actual reason was that no one but Esme understood her system of communication with all the once-a-year church people in the city who came to the candlelight service. And Esme claimed to not be able to get out of her driveway. When Bob offered to pick her up, she said her pipes had frozen and she wasn't able to shower.

April grabbed his phone before he offered up the March family bathroom. "She's perfectly capable of getting out of her driveway. She's from Minnesota, for God's sake. She just doesn't want to be bothered. And I don't believe her pipes are frozen. She lives in a condo."

By December 24th, the main roads and the busiest of the side roads were cleared, either officially or by drivers who had grown up in Minnesota. Christmas lights were back on in most parts of the city. What remained of the storm was the lovely snow. Snowmen appeared in every yard where jack-o'-lanterns had glowed two months prior. Orange cones and official signs closed off steep streets that were then taken over by sleds and children in bright colored coats.

The sanctuary was packed by eleven o'clock on Christmas Eve for the lessons and carols service. It hadn't changed in fifty years. The grand finale was always "Silent Night: A Dramatic Treatment." Everyone, even children, was allowed a white candle with a drip shield. People on the end of each row of pews lit their candles, and the flame was passed down the row. As soon as all the candles were lit, the hall lights were turned off.

Throughout the lighting of the candles, Jeff tooled away on the organ, playing a medley of carols into which he always managed to insert reverent arrangements of "Santa Baby" or "I Saw Mommy Kissing Santa Claus." ("So lovely to hear some of the old carols we don't always hear," Mrs. Johansen commented.) When the hall lights went down, Jeff launched the last two lines of "Silent Night," that is to say, the "heavenly peace" lines, the screechy one and the calm one. It was the cue for Brianna and Amanda to enter the choir loft from the greenroom (the vestry) and stand ready to sign.

The door from the vestry opened and Amanda poked her head out. "Jeff," she hissed. "Brianna won't do it."

Jeff grinned. "Tell her she has to."

He repeated the heavenly peaces.

"She feels sick. She can't stand up."

Jeff modulated to a higher key, which prevented everyone from beginning to sing "Silent Night," which was just as well because the choir had gotten the giggles.

"Does she want me to help?" Nicholas, in the bass section, stood next to the vestry door, from which came a strangled but emphatic "No!"

"You do it yourself," Jeff said to Amanda.

"I can't. I don't really know how. I just copy Brianna."

Jeff was laughing as he came round to the heavenly peaces in the higher key while all through the church, paraffin dripped solemnly down 250 white candles. He moved skillfully back to the friendly key and signaled Chalice. The choir got hold of itself in time for Chalice's downbeat and finally everyone was singing, but, sadly, without the signers.

They sang all three verses. The first verse was always the most robust, the second and third suffering some attrition. The more unchurched one is, the less likely to know all the verses, which were hard to read; Esme had crammed them in a small font at the end of the order of service, not wanting to have to print another sheet of paper and not willing to edit anything that came before.

The congregation left the church in little clumps of people, still holding their lit candles, twinkling like tiny stars moving among the mounds of snow. Brianna made a miraculous recovery. She and Nicholas exited through the church office, which was cloudy with cigarette smoke. Esme, sitting at the desk, dropped her cigarette in a drawer and slammed it shut.

"Merry Christmas," she said brightly.

Jeff pushed the magic stop on the organ that transferred the sound to the chimes in the church tower. "Silent Night" chimed at midnight throughout the neighborhood. Then the world went silent except for the crunch of footsteps in snow and the occasional curse when someone slipped on ice.

Chapter Twenty

Advancing the Retreat

The flames must have burned in secret for a long time. By the time the fire trucks put out the fire, the sanctuary, offices, and smaller rooms were hollowed out. Most of the new wing was gone. The round room was standing, albeit singed around the edges and without a roof. The plastic labyrinth was seared onto the floor.

Rambles, sitting in a front window across the street, had watched the fire all night, the only living creature who witnessed the whole thing. Bob March had made the 9-1-1 call in the early hours of Christmas morning. The commotion of the trucks awakened the surrounding houses, including the Martins and briefly exciting Chase, who thought Santa Claus had crashed in their neighborhood.

At dawn the gaping mess was exposed. The neighborhood came out in full force, still in pajamas and bathrobes, to huddle and stare. Church members appeared seemingly en masse and without any help from Esme's communication system. They stood awkwardly around Victor and Kimberly, both of whom looked dazed.

The fire investigator held up the remains of one of Corinne's pillow lumps. "It seems as though one of these things caught fire from a candle that wasn't completely extinguished. A second fire was started by a cigarette left burning in a drawer in the church office."

Kimberly pronounced a word no one had ever heard her use.

April, standing at her front window, in the warmth of her home, had an uncharacteristically charitable idea. First she called Libby and Kay. Then she roused Nicholas out of bed and told him Christmas had been canceled.

"Well, actually, not canceled. Christmas is being rerouted to its original purpose. Or something like that," she said enigmatically.

Kay arrived with her giant church potluck water heater and all the Christmas cookies and pastries she had in her house. She made coffee, cut up pastries, and arranged plates of cookies.

April handed Nicholas a snow shovel and set him to shoveling out her labyrinth. She walked ahead of him, leaving footprints to outline the circuits and loop-backs.

Libby and Callie arrived. Libby had lettered a large sign that read "Labyrinth open for Christmas Day." April pinned the sign to the top of the arbor and propped open the front gate. Then she took two mugs of coffee across the street and handed them to Victor and Kimberly.

"Come in out of the cold," she said.

The End
(for now)

Thanks to:

Dana Caldart for information about fires

Gwen Howell for dressing everyone and giving them cars

Jennifer D. Munro for her gracious, tactful, and cheerful editing, especially the tedious copy-editing

Julie Welch for all things Hispanic

Nina Christensen for her recipe for Old Fashioneds and for reading the first fifty pages fifty times

Nina (again), Anna Ellermeier and Susan Towle for their eleventh hour proofing

Tommie Eckert and Matthew Lyon for their company and generosity on Whidbey Island, where most of this novel was written

All my friends who let me use their names

My students and choirs, who Give Me Ideas.

About the Author

Born in Seattle, Washington and a Whitman College graduate, ELENA LOUISE RICHMOND writes and teaches singing, piano and watercolor in her Local Dilettante Studio in the Crown Hill neighborhood of Seattle.

www.elenalouiserichmond.com

CPSIA information can be obtained
at www.ICGtesting.com
Printed in the USA
FSHW011252310321
80035FS